THE TALE OF CAPRI

The Tale of Capri

A Story Inspired by MerMay

By Kathleen Solis

The Capri Saga

Book 1

ISBN
979-8-9954655-0-8 (e-book)
979-8-9954655-1-5 (paperback)
979-8-9954655-2-2 (hardcover)

Library of Congress Control Number: 2026909693
Second Edition

Cover Design and Interior Formatting by 100 Covers
Original illustrations by Kathleen Solis

Visit the author's website at www.kathleensolis.com
This book is typeset in Palatino Linotype and Brilon.

Dedicated to Tom Bancroft
for inspiring artists and creatives
around the world with a love for mermaids,
art, animation, and self-improvement.

In special memory of
Klaus Cuthbert and Don Rorschach.
May your names be remembered
in the pages of this book.
Rest in peace.

Experience *The Tale of Capri* on audiobook, read by the author.

The audiobook includes an original instrumental theme written and produced exclusively for *The Capri Saga*.

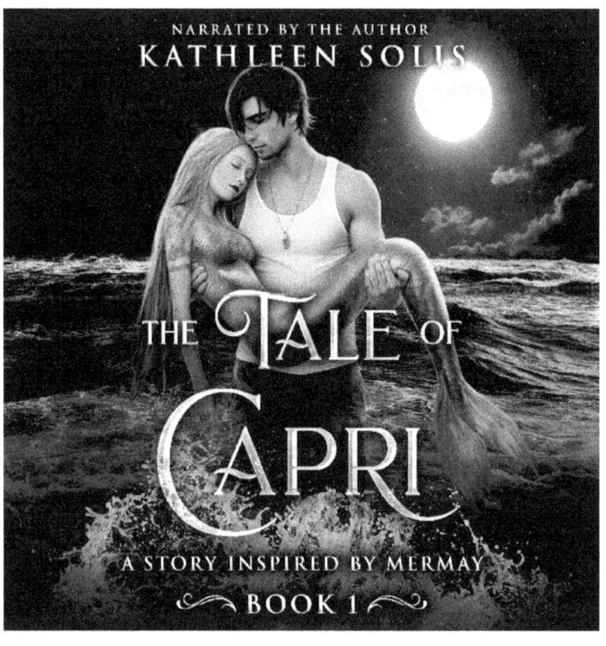

Contents

AUTHOR'S NOTE: MERMAY ORIGINS

The Tale of Capri began as a series of fun, experimental drawings that followed prompts during MerMay 2019—a month-long challenge created by former Disney animator Tom Bancroft. The challenge, which still runs annually as of this writing, entails drawing a mermaid every day during the month of May in order to improve one's drawing and animation skills. I've been an artist for about as long as I've been fascinated with mermaids, so naturally, I had to participate in the challenge. I had an image stuck in my head of a lifeguard rescuing a mermaid, and I just had to draw it. I came to like their design so much that a short story sequence spawned from the drawing. Following the official prompt list, I wound up creating a story that was told over the course of the entire month.

Although I'd argue that the story wrote itself, there are some scenes in the book which are inspired by real-life stories and scenarios from divers I've spoken with, such as the real-life ghost nets that entangle sea creatures (and endanger divers!) and a too-close-for-comfort encounter between a diver and a moray eel.

The original story I created was well-received. Towards the end of May, there was enough of a demand for the story to become a published book, and so from there, I expanded the story and character development, publishing it with the original illustrations.

When I revisited the book seven years later in 2026, I found that the original story was a mere skeleton for the story that deserved to be told. Thus, the second edition was born. A handful of grayscale renderings of the original illustrations made during the 2019 MerMay challenge can be found at the back of this book.

I hope you enjoy this story as much as I enjoyed discovering it day by day during MerMay 2019.

CHAPTER 1

SAVING CAPRI

A searing pain crept up her aqua tail. Capri looked down to see a thin red cloud trailing behind her as she sped toward the ocean's surface.

No! It got me, she thought.

Terror had driven away any perception of pain. Now that she'd created distance between her and the deep-sea attack only moments earlier, she was beginning to feel faint. Her body was beginning to succumb to the injury. She only had a few minutes to make it to the surface before being rendered unconscious. At that point, she would be at the mercy of any predators who might pick up the scent of her blood. The only safe place she could think to escape to was the coast, either in a sea cave or the tide pools next to a beach where she knew the humans liked to play. She grimaced at the thought.

I can't risk being seen by curious humans. And I certainly will not *swim through that filthy plastic water around the tide pools. I'd sooner take my chances with the sea.*

She wasn't sure if her paranoid mind was playing tricks on her or if she was hallucinating from the loss of blood, but the hazy silhouette of a large shark had begun to emerge in the near distance.

Then again…

In spite of her dizziness, she swam as far and as hard as she could, taking the long route past the crowded beach to avoid being seen. The ocean began to spin as she reached the rocky coastline. She could hardly swim in a straight line as the life drained out of her. The distant shape of the shark loomed in the near distance.

No time to make it to the caves. Ugh, I guess I'm doing this, she thought, looking up at the thick ceiling of garbage that blocked out the sunlight. A primal survival instinct pressed her forward.

She held her breath, squeezing her eyes shut as she ascended through the clouded water. Every plastic particle stuck to her scales as she passed through the suffocating layer of debris. When she surfaced, she gulped in the pure spring air. Her fingers were so weak, she could barely keep her grip on the rocks as she heaved herself up out of the water and collapsed into the tide pools. She was grateful for the somewhat cleaner water that rinsed her scales of the excess debris clinging to her. Her tail stung in the exposed air. It felt heavier, too. She allowed it to flop into the shallow water which barely covered it. Despite the ringing in her ears, she thought she heard screams along the beach about a shark.

I'm still too close. It didn't matter anymore. A hissing ocean consumed her hearing. The sky spun as the burning sun smeared across her vision. Then darkness fell.

It was the first day of May. Eden hadn't expected a shark sighting on the beach quite this early in the season, but it was inevitable. After he had finished his lifeguard report, Eden was relieved to be wrapping up for the day as he drove his truck along the sunny coastline, stopping periodically to post shark advisory signs to close the beach for the day.

As he posted his final advisory, right by the entrance nearest the sea cliffs, something prompted him to look toward the tide pools. The late afternoon sun was still sparkling brightly on the water, but to his surprise, he could just make out the vague shape of a figure down there. It was so subtle, anyone would have missed it.

After roping off the final beach entrance, Eden collected his first aid bag before making his way down toward the tidepools, glancing about to see if anyone else was present. A small smile tugged at the corners of his lips. It was just him and the untainted sounds of the ocean—just as he liked it.

Even as he neared his destination, he couldn't quite make out what was in the water, if it was even there anymore. He might have taken his eyes off the tide pools for a few moments here and there to watch his footing, but something urged him to continue his investigation.

As he clambered down over the first of the jagged rocks leading down to the tide pools, a figure broke through the shallow water. No loud splashes or gasps, just rising to sit up amidst stray bits of floating refuse. The sight startled him so much that he nearly stumbled, but a sharp exhale escaped him instead.

He froze, staring on in silence. There was no obvious distress in the figure's movements, which was strange given that they had been submerged this whole time. He held back a moment to see what would happen.

The figure parted a thick curtain of long, wet aqua hair, revealing the fragile shape of a young woman. Something was rather disturbing about her though. Her skin looked as though she had already drowned and had become the sea itself.

Eden still didn't know who or what he was looking at, but the distress in her groans moved him to offer his aid. Cautious not to surprise her, he let his shoes scrape audibly against the rock, followed by clearing his throat softly.

It must have been loud enough for the young woman to hear because, like a startled animal, she whirled to face him, eyes wide, scrunching her knees up to her chest. Something was definitely strange about her skin—no, scales! They seemed to cover her entire body from her head to her… no, it couldn't be.

Eden stifled a gasp because the woman's legs weren't legs at all. His jaw hung open as he realized that he had just locked eyes with—he couldn't believe he was thinking this—a *mermaid*?

The human and the mermaid stared at each other for what felt like ages, waiting for the other to make the first move.

When he found his words, Eden stammered, "Y-you're wounded!"

The mermaid hazarded only the briefest of glances at her tail, which was still bleeding. "Stay away! Don't hurt me!"

"It's alright," he said, softening his voice and raising his empty hands to sell his harmlessness. "My name is Eden. I'm a lifeguard. I—I can help."

He descended into the tide pool and made his way toward her, but the mermaid recoiled, prompting him to stop.

"Please, may I help you?" he said warmly. Every movement slowed as he bent into a squat. "It's alright. I won't hurt you." He extended a hand.

The mermaid was quiet for a long while. Her eyes darted warily between his face, his hand, his legs, the bag on his back, and his face again. When it was clear that he would do nothing until she answered, she hardened her face and gave him a curt, "No."

Disappointment replaced the kind smile on his face. The amount of blood clouding the water near her tail urged him to stay and offer aid, but he couldn't force his help onto anyone if they voluntarily refused it. It pained him to climb back out of the tide pools. He'd barely gone a few steps before he heard a distressed whimper from behind him.

"Wait!"

He gasped, putting a hand to his chest as he felt something stir inside of him, the likes of which he could only describe as a splashing ocean. It crashed desperately against the sea wall of his rib cage, pulling at him like the mermaid's cry had reached into his soul. Unsure of what to make of the sensation, he looked back to see her faltering, growing pale as she clutched her tail.

"Please," she strained in a half-sob. "Help me."

Without a second thought, Eden scurried back down to the tide pool just as her supporting arm buckled.

"Woah, woah, easy there," he said, catching her from behind her shoulders. Her head lazed back as she fell unconscious. He was surprised at how light her body felt in his arms, resembling the near weightlessness of one carried underwater. "It's okay, I've got you."

He knelt down to better position himself beside her in the water, supporting her neck and shoulders as he did. Up close, the laceration looked gnarly, but it didn't appear as deep as he'd initially thought. Given the darker color and slow, flowy nature of the wound, he identified it as a venous bleed—urgent but not life-threatening despite the intimidating red in the water.

The mermaid was so limp that, for a moment, he worried that she might have died right there in his arms. He proceeded with emergency protocol. Based on her humanoid top half, he reasoned to check for her pulse as he would on any human. Courteously wetting his hands before handling her scales, he felt her wrist and beneath her neck, which lacked any gills, much to his surprise.

Why is that surprising? he thought. This was a mythical creature who shouldn't exist. How should he expect anything?

A slow but sure pulse thrummed against his fingers in both places.

So far so good, he thought. He brought his ear close to her face tilting her head back and opening her jaw to listen for signs of life. Placing his cheek next to her striking red lips, he tried feeling for her breath. Silence. Turning his head to look down towards her tail, he rested his free hand on her stomach, albeit with slight hesitation against the unusual texture of scales in place of skin. He focused against the churning of the nearby ocean, searching for any corresponding rising and falling of her body with each breath.

Please breathe. Come on, breathe!

There it was. His hand rose with her belly in a long, slow, quiet inhale. His breath unconsciously fell into rhythm with hers, syncing with the pulse of the surf as it crept up toward the shore, suspended itself to a whisper on the sandy banks, and withdrew once again. The feathery puff of her exhale tickled his cheek as he sighed in relief. She would live.

"Let's get you to a better spot," he said, scanning the rocks up the shore for a better place to tend to her wounds than in bloody, dirty water. He gingerly slid one hand under her tail and the other around her scaled back, lifting her with ease. "You'll be alright. I've got you," he said.

When her head lolled against his shoulder, that odd feeling of the sea in his chest rose up again, something akin to the small but desperate lapping of a wave longing to touch the top of a sea cliff. Only his unspeakable pining for the sea had ever matched such a sensation. He regarded her unconscious figure. Surely, she was the source of this strange feeling inside him. But how?

As he set her down to recline against a smooth set of rocks, he paused when he laid eyes on her face, pain etched across it. The reality that he'd found a mermaid—of all creatures!—hit him.

"They're real?" he whispered.

While he placed pressure on the wound with fresh gauze, he ran a curious finger down a few of her scales, confirming the reality of his unusual circumstances. Their smooth texture was as real as any fish he had ever handled. His gaze traveled up to her face again. She was a stunning vision out of a long-forgotten dream. By his estimation, she must have been a few years younger than him, probably around eighteen or nineteen at best.

The shimmering greens and blues of her scales created stunning marbled patterns over the pale seafoam-green ones, dressing her long, slender body from head to tail in a mesmerizing garb that only the sea could have painted. The longer he stared at her, the more Eden felt the reverence of cradling a corporeal embodiment of a hurting ocean which had fashioned itself into the form of a beautiful, delicate mermaid.

As the bleeding came to a stop, he shot a glance up near the obscured roadway where he had parked his truck. As far as he could tell, no one had seen them. There was no way he was speaking of this to anyone. He didn't believe in fate, and he wasn't about to entertain it, but here he was, caring for a creature that he'd passively fancied might be real once, long ago.

He sighed. "Well, this'll be interesting."

CHAPTER 2

THE LIFEGUARD

The whispering of the ocean was the first thing that crept into Capri's consciousness. Then the feeling of the sun's warmth and the hardness of something flat and stony behind her. Her tail throbbed. She opened her eyes to see the young lifeguard kneeling on the ground before her, cleaning and tending to her wound. The instinct to recoil at the disgusting touch of a human was fierce, but she was far too weak to move. How had she cracked under the pressure of desperation and begged for a *human's* help? A sick feeling arose in her stomach.

"It's all right. You're doing great," said Eden when she flinched. "I've cleaned the wound, and I'm bandaging it now." His warm baritone had a strange, calming effect on her, melting the tension in her shoulders.

"How are you feeling?" he asked, unwrapping a clean packet of gauze.

She had already spoken to the human once, but doing so was as unnatural as being out of water. *Not much point in delaying the inevitable.* "I'm…alive."

"Alright. That's a good thing."

Capri didn't answer as her body seized against a searing flash through her tail. She squeezed her eyes, groaning and gritting her teeth against it.

"I'm sorry, this might hurt," said Eden, wincing along with her as he adjusted her tail, propping it over his lap to create enough space to wrap the wound. "I'll work quickly. Just take a few breaths. It'll help with the pain."

Her inhale was sharp and her exhale ragged.

"Easy now. I'll do it with you. Slow breath in." He placed a hand on his own chest, miming an exaggerated motion of breathing.

The mermaid nodded. The air quivered from her lips in her attempt to match his breath.

"There you go. In…and breathe out. Nice and steady." His breath was a slow, audible *whoosh,* similar to the rush of the nearby surf.

The pained creases on the mermaid's face softened.

"That's right. Don't hold your breath. Just keep breathing. Nice and easy," said Eden. He noted the movements of her rib cage, searching for signs of gills along her sides. Nothing presented itself. Putting his curiosities aside, he gave the mermaid some time to find her rhythm before attempting to speak again. "Can you tell me how this happened?"

A wary silence staggered her brief responses. "A colossal squid. One of its hooks got me."

"The spinning hooks on its tentacles?"

Capri sat up a bit, surprised. "You know of these creatures?"

"Very little. I've lived next to the ocean all my life, and I've studied marine creatures, or at least whatever there is to learn about them. I'm sorry to hear about that encounter. Deep sea, huh? It must have been scary."

"It was."

"I'm glad you made it out of there alive." He spoke as naturally as if she were the same species as him. She didn't know what to make of it.

"I didn't like coming to the tide pools though," she said, hugging herself.

"Oh? Why is that?"

A bitterness filled her eyes as she recalled her agonizing ascent through the polluted water in vivid detail. "Filth. Refuse." Her jaw clenched. "Plastic."

Eden paused, sensing her pain, which was becoming less physical and more emotional. Whatever she had gone through near the tide pools might have been more traumatic than this supposed colossal squid attack.

"I'm sorry to hear that," he said.

She flinched when the pain in her tail yanked her out of her thoughts, studying Eden as he worked. The shape of his legs was so alien up close. The thin layer of moisture shimmering on his exposed arms and face puzzled her too. How could he become wet when he was nowhere near water? He was unlike anything she had imagined humans to be, and yet the familiarity of the shape of his upper half, which was fashioned similarly to that of her own species, was mildly reassuring. She could only look for so long in the bright sun before the harsh white and red of his lifeguard uniform made the backs of her eyes throb.

*An actual human…*touching *me,* she thought. The more his hands worked on her, the less revolted she became. There was a strange comfort in his touch, something as foreign as it was familiar. *Who* is *this human?*

At length, she dared herself to ask some questions of her own to distract from the burning in her tail and her nagging nausea. "So, you say you're a lifeguard. What is that?"

"I make sure people are safe when they visit the beach, and I help them if they're hurt, kind of like you."

"Where does a lifeguard live? You don't live in the tide pools, do you?"

He stifled a chuckle. "No, but I do visit them sometimes. I live in a house on land."

"A house?"

"It's… Huh, how do I say this? It's like a large box made from wood, brick, or stone."

"You live in a box? Do you hunt fish?"

Eden shrugged. "I'm not one for fishing. Not as fun as swimming. But I have assisted at the aquarium where I've helped rescue and rehabilitate wildlife—" He stopped when he caught himself rambling words that she probably didn't understand, which was confirmed by her knitted brow. "I help fish recover when they get hurt."

"Oh. Makes sense," she said, watching him tie off the bandage. She winced as he lowered her tail from his lap.

"There. I think we're done," he said, wiping his hands on his swim trunks.

The mermaid ran a curious finger over the secure bandage, testing its edges. She shot him a guarded glare. "This will come off, right?"

"Of course," said Eden. "I'd recommend leaving it on for a few hours until the bleeding stops. It'll take some time to heal. For now, take it easy and avoid flexing your tail too much."

It was strange speaking about injured tails instead of limbs. What kind of a fever dream was this?

The rush of the afternoon waves reminded Eden of what needed to happen next. "I figure…out there is home. But I wouldn't feel right sending you out there, especially after the shark sighting earlier."

"So there *was* a shark?"

"Yeah, maybe an hour ago. I was closing up the beach and posting shark advisories in this area when I had the feeling to check the tide pools. That's when I found you."

Horrible images flashed through Capri's head—the filth near the tide pools, the sharp, spinning hooks of the colossal squid's tentacles, and a horrible net…

She shuddered. *No, I can't go back.* The mercy of the shark sounded more certain than being able to survive in the sea with an injury this large. The throb in her tail reminded her that she was as good as dead on her own.

"Let's see..." said Eden, rubbing his chin. "Maybe I could take you to the sea caves near the—"

"Don't leave me," she blurted. She could hardly believe her own words. "I'm—you're the only one who can help me. I can't go back out there, not yet."

The desperation in her eyes was difficult to ignore, and what tragically beautiful eyes they were, as rich and as pained as the sea.

"I—oh man, this is crazy," said Eden, raking his fingers through his dark hair. He was trained for the unexpected, but this was too much. What was he supposed to do with a *mermaid*? He was no medical professional or marine expert, but his limited knowledge in both fields was the only chance this mermaid had at survival and recovery. It would weigh on him if he didn't do something, especially after what he'd done to the sea last year...

He stood, looking at the mermaid's bandaged tail, then at her frightened face. *I* owe *her this,* he thought.

Capri watched him pace back and forth, listening to him mutter something about closed beaches, nighttime, curious teenagers, and urban legends.

"Alright, listen," he said finally, kneeling before her at eye level. "I—oh, this is crazy—I have a saltwater pool at my house. It's probably safer than the ocean or the tide pools right now, and it's hidden away from everyone. No one would disturb you, I promise. I can monitor your wound, and you can stay until you feel well enough to return to the sea. Alternatively, I could leave you someplace similar to where I found you and do my best to check in on you. It's your choice."

The mermaid thought to take her chances by the sea caves, but only briefly. She dreaded anyone else finding her there. She'd been fortunate enough to encounter this young lifeguard. He seemed friendly enough. Come to think of it, he'd refrained from pressuring her toward *any* decision. A creature like him must be worth trusting, even temporarily.

"I…think I'd be willing to try it, human Eden."

"Please, call me Eden," he said. "Okay, I'm going to pick you up now. I'll take you back to my truck, and we'll get you settled down at the pool." He carefully looped an arm under her tail and around her back to pick her up. "Are you ready?"

The mermaid nodded. She clutched his tank top at the unfamiliar sensation of gravity on land as he lifted her, but the feeling of his arms around her was as soothing to her nerves as his voice. It wasn't supposed to feel like this.

"By the way, I never got your name," said Eden as he began his hike up the beach.

"Capri. I am Capri."

"Capri," he repeated. "Beautiful name."

A sparkle lit up her eyes when he said her name, and the nausea in her stomach began to subside.

As they reached the top of the beach, she pressed herself against him nervously when they neared a large, intimidating metal machine.

"It's alright," he assured her. "It's only my truck."

"A truck?" she said, trying to keep her voice steady.

"Um…it's a machine that transports me around land."

"Like a land boat?"

"Eh…something like that, yes. Don't worry, it's nothing to be afraid of."

Eden awkwardly opened the door with one hand and set the mermaid in the passenger seat, but he didn't position her tail forward just yet.

"Sorry, give me a second," he said as he shuffled a few loose items from the floorboards.

Capri grimaced at the handful of plastic cups, pieces of paper, a crumpled paper bag, and other bits of garbage that littered the floorboards. The only item that held her attention was a black bar of metal. It sounded heavy as he placed it in the empty cup holder beside her. She scrutinized it while he angled her tail fins into place to sit in the seat properly.

"It's a tool," he said, climbing into the driver's seat.

Something about the object looked vaguely familiar, but her anxiety prevented her from exploring it further when Eden's hand came reaching across her shoulder, bringing a long flat strap across her body.

"What are you doing?" she cried, seizing his wrist. "Trying to tie me down?"

Her sudden willingness to handle him surprised him. "It's a safety belt. It keeps you secure while we drive."

"Tying me down keeps me safe?"

"I-it's not so much tying you down as it is securing you in place. I have one too, see?" he said, reaching for his own seat belt and buckling himself in. "They can easily be undone. I assure you, you're not trapped."

He demonstrated by unbuckling the belt and re-buckling it on himself. Capri eyed the strap across his chest and lap apprehensively. Human logic was so strange. Already, she wanted to get out of the truck, but dreaded going back to the beach.

"Very well," she said after a bit. She held her breath as Eden slowly crossed the belt over her and it clicked into place. The belt didn't constrict the top of her tail too firmly, but the strap across her upper torso was a bit unpleasant. She twisted uncomfortably.

"It's a short drive, I promise," said Eden. "We'll be out of here quickly."

Chapter 3

The Garden of Eden

Between hearing the mermaid's gasps as the vehicle roared to life and watching her grip the seat with remarkable strength whenever they came upon a bump in the road, Eden patiently drove home, taking care to drive slowly so as not to frighten her more than she already was.
In time, Capri became secretly grateful for the safety belt, which had started to feel more like a lifeline than a trap. It was only a few minutes' drive, but it felt so much longer to her. She was quite relieved when the vehicle came to a stop in front of a tall, dark, pristine wooden gate at the end of the street across from the sea. Eden unbuckled both himself and the mermaid, who failed to suppress her relief. It was a good thing they'd arrived when they did, because her scales were beginning to dry out.

Splashing his hands and forearms with water from his canteen, Eden scooped her up from the passenger seat and carried her down a short stone path toward the gate. Through it was a large, rectangular swimming pool surrounded by a lush garden. A huge, slatted roof covered the entire courtyard like a cozy, intimate canopy. Over the pool area was a wide opening like an oculus, revealing the clear, late afternoon sky.

Eden squatted, setting Capri into the pool. The moment she was in the water, she wriggled out of his hands to the pool's center like a fish escaping a fisherman's hands, disappearing beneath the surface. Eden couldn't make out what she was doing because her movements continuously agitated the pool's surface.

Her scales probably needed the water, he guessed. He pulled up a lawn chair and watched for any signs of distress or pain as she adjusted to the space.

After about twenty minutes, Capri's head broke noiselessly through the surface near the center of the pool. She found Eden waiting patiently with his hands folded between his knees.

"How's the water?" he asked.

She didn't answer right away. The briny taste of the saltwater was significantly less intense than the ocean, but it had been enough to calm her senses. Her gaze wandered around the pool, taking in the canopy of plants surrounding her. Green ivy crawled up the sides of the fence. Red and orange hibiscus blossoms were in full bloom in semi-recessed pots on the sides of the pool so that the flowers were nearly level with the water. Vines crept across the courtyard's slatted ceiling to meet the rectangular oculus, and other greenery tumbled over the sides like botanical waterfalls. She'd never seen so much velvety green vegetation, save perhaps a few coastal trees or grass from a safe distance.

"It's fine," she answered finally. "Does anyone else live here?"

"No, it's just me. I mean, I have neighbors on that side of the fence, but they're pretty quiet. They're out of town this week though, and I'm not expecting any visitors, so you won't be bothered here."

"I see." Her eyes traveled around the canopy, studying this strange new world until her gaze settled back onto the human. "*This* is your home?"

"It is. Well, *that* is my house," he said, pointing to a structure that connected to the pool area. "Inside the house are a couple of rooms; spaces where I can eat and sleep. But I like to spend much of my time here."

"I can see why," she said, wincing whenever she moved her tail too much. "Do you care for these plants yourself?"

"Every one of them."

"They must like you to grow so nicely for you."

Eden grinned at the observation. "I do my best to take care of them."

"Will you take care of *me*?" Worry filled her expression as if contemplating abandonment.

"Of course," he said, standing. "I'll do what I can to help you recover. Maybe I can start with the basics. Can I get you anything to eat? Er, what do mermaids eat?"

"I eat mollusks and sea lettuce. But I can also eat shrimp, crab, and lobster."

"Hmmm…I'll be back." He disappeared into the house for a minute and returned with a plastic container in one hand and a sealed plastic bag which crackled in the other.

He hadn't gone five steps from the house when Capri backed away to the far edge of the pool.

Eden raised an eyebrow. "What?"

"What are those?" she demanded.

"Oh these? It's some food for you to eat."

As he opened the container, the sound of tearing, snapping plastic ripped across the pool's surface. The mermaid flinched.

Eden noticed. "Is there a problem?"

"I don't eat plastic," said Capri, raising a corner of her upper lip in disgust.

"Oh! No, you misunderstand. There's shrimp *inside* the container. I'm opening it for you."

"I won't eat something that's been in *plastic,*" she said, as if the very word possessed a foul flavor.

"Oh," said Eden, dropping his shoulders. "It's all I have. I-I'd brought you shrimp and some dried nori."

"What's nori?"

"It's dried seaweed."

Her eyes darted between the two items he'd set on the ground. "Which one is that?"

Eden held up the bag which crackled again as he moved it.

She shivered at the harsh sound. "I'm not eating that. I'd sooner starve."

His face fell. Thinking back, Eden recalled her mentioning plastic when he was tending to her earlier on the beach. He guessed she might have a negative association with it based on a previous experience.

Pressing his lips together, he contemplated his options. "What if I lay out the shrimp on the side of the pool? Without the plastic."

"Which one is the shrimp?"

Eden opted to point at the container rather than touch it.

"Can I see one?"

As quietly as possible, Eden snapped the plastic container apart, pulling out a single gray shrimp with neither head nor legs.

Capri's mouth watered at the sight of the familiar food. Her head tilted as she considered it, weighing her growing hunger against her hatred of the makeup of its container.

When she didn't say anything, Eden broke the long silence. "Uh, how about I run back to the beach to collect some kelp? Can you eat that? There's always some that's washed up."

Capri nodded.

"In the meantime, I'll lay the shrimp out for you in case you change your mind. Is that fair?"

She chewed on her lip and nodded again.

Eden laid out six shrimp beside the pool's edge and collected the container and bag to return them to the house. Capri was still pressed against the far end of the pool when he came back outside.

"I'll be back in a few minutes," he said. "The beach is down the road, so I won't be gone long. The gate is high and the neighborhood is fairly quiet, so like I said before, no one will see you or bother you. Will you be okay until then?"

He almost missed her acknowledging nod as she lowered her head into the water until only the top of her head and eyes were visible.

"Alright. I'll be back in a few. I promise."

Eden would have easily walked to the beach as was his custom, but he took his truck for transporting the kelp to avoid curious stares that might raise suspicion. As he rinsed and collected a few short ropes of kelp in the surf, he scanned the horizon, half hoping that he might catch a glimpse of another mer. He berated himself when he realized that he hadn't asked Capri if she'd been going about solo or if she had been with a group of merfolk who might be searching for her. It had been lost in the flurry of questions he had, but in the short time he'd known her, she hadn't been one for talking as much.

She'll tell me if and when she's ready, he thought. *My only job is to care for her until she recovers and can make it on her own. No need to get too curious or attached. She probably won't even be around for very long.*

The very thought brought a tinge of sadness, but he shrugged the feeling aside as he loaded the kelp into his truck and made his way back home.

Upon his return, the shrimp had vanished from the poolside, and the mermaid looked more relaxed. She craned her neck as he hauled in the kelp stalks.

"Will this work for you?" asked Eden.

"Nicely," she said.

That was the first time he had seen the ghost of a smile tug at the corners of her mouth. Eden unloaded the ropes of kelp and laid them out for her. She plucked one of the tough leaves off with surprising ease and began nibbling on it gratefully upon tasting the familiar sharp brine of the sea.

Eden sat back to give her some space. "How was the shrimp?"

She stopped mid-bite, giving him an almost guilty look. She bit off a piece of kelp. "Mmhmm," she said with a repetitive nod, keeping her eyes on the kelp.

"You can tell me if you didn't like them, you know," said Eden.

She swallowed her fresh food. "No, I did like them. They were colder than I prefer. The kelp is good though."

She took another bite, chewed quietly for a minute, and swallowed before adding, "I don't mean to sound ungrateful. You're sharing your own food with me and went out of your way to fetch me kelp. You have my thanks."

"You're welcome," said Eden.

Capri then held out a leaf. "Can I offer you one?"

"Oh, those were meant for you," he said, surprised by her gesture.

"It's the least I can offer."

"Thanks, but I'm fine. I, uh, I don't eat kelp anyway."

"You're not just saying that to be polite, are you? You can tell me if you don't like it, you know."

Eden chuckled at her imitation of him. *Now we're getting somewhere.* "No. Honest. I don't eat kelp. It's probably too tough and fibrous for me. But thanks, Capri."

She perked up at the use of her name. He might try saying it more often.

After dinner and a short workout, Eden went back outside for his usual evening routine of tending the garden. A tentative silence hung in the air as he worked on the vines. Once or twice, he would cast a glance into the deepest part of the pool where Capri was hunkered down. In spite of his curiosity, he thought it wiser to give her what little privacy he could offer her. *She'll come up to tell me if she needs something.*

Every once in a while, the mermaid would silently surface while he had his back turned and observe him. His gloved hands worked with care and gentleness among the greenery and blossoms. Whenever she thought he might turn, she would duck back under water as noiselessly as when she had surfaced.

Eden could usually sense when she was watching, but he didn't mind. It was kind of nice having a guest over for a change. It had been a while since he'd had anyone besides family stay overnight, so he was glad to play the role of host. *At least this time, no one can try anything stupid on me,* he thought as the specter of an unpleasant memory drifted through his mind. He shook the thought away, resuming his gardening work.

As the rectangular oculus above changed color with the setting sun, lights began to turn on in the courtyard. String lights adorned the top edges of the entire fence, illuminating the garden's beauty, even in the twilight hour. The vines weaving at the top of the latticed roof were contoured by soft uplights. Even the pool was illuminated by a dim gradient of light cascading along its walls.

When the last of the hibiscus plants was watered, Eden turned his attention to Capri, who had given up hiding underwater. He delighted in her wide-eyed wonder as she drank in the tranquility of the evening paradise he'd crafted for her.

"How's the tail?" he asked, taking off his gardening gloves.

She blinked, breaking out of her trance. "Better than before. But you were right. The bandage *can* come off. It's loose right now. Is that bad?"

"Oh. Um, hang on, I'll be right back." Eden ran inside the house and returned with a red medical bag. "I can check on the wound and apply a new dressing, then I can check on it again in the morning. How's that sound?"

"Okay."

"Right, well, um..." He hadn't considered how he might tend to her in the water. He paced to the edge of the pool nearest to his house. "Let's see, how about you come over here."

Capri met him at a convenient, low, underwater ledge. She sat herself upon it, but her tail remained submerged. The water came only halfway up her torso. This still wasn't optimal.

Eden squatted, shaking his head. "Hmm, let's see. How about—"

The mermaid gripped the edge of the pool and pushed herself up out of the water to sit beside him.

Eden's eyes widened. "Oh, well...um, that works."

Grimacing, Capri lifted her tail out of the water and flopped it down with a limp, wet smack on the smooth concrete, narrowly missing his hand with her fins. "Sorry, that was harder than I meant," she said through gritted teeth. Managing her tail outside of the water was still so foreign. "It still hurts. Is, uh...is this okay?"

"Uh, y-yeah," stammered Eden. Seeing her outside of the water was still so jarring when he'd grown accustomed to seeing just her head and shoulders sticking out of the water. Using a pair of shears, he carefully removed the loose dressings from around her tail.

"Seems the bleeding has stopped. That's a good sign," he said reassuringly. "It's clotting well. No infection as far as I can tell. I'll keep an eye on it over the next couple of days. As for pain, it's probably going to be very sore, but if you start feeling unusually warm or experience any dizziness or nausea, I need to know. Can you do that for me?"

"I can," she said.

"Other than some pain, how are you feeling?" he asked.

Any further words drained back into his throat as he laid eyes on her elegant frame. If her scales had resembled the sparkling sea in the daylight, the warm evening lighting of the courtyard costumed her body with sharply contrasting scale patterns like an exotic gown against the backdrop of the garden. It was like being lost in a vaguely familiar dream.

"Better," said Capri, feeling his gaze. And yet, as much as she despised humans, she was strangely unbothered by it. There was a certain reassurance behind his eyes that quieted her turbulent spirit. How did a *human* have the ability to persuade her to relax her guard, even just a little bit?

Eden cleared his throat. "Good. I-I'll bandage this again for the night and check on it tomorrow morning."

Capri watched silently as he irrigated her wound. She was intrigued by how his entire being was completely oriented toward her care. Even his tongue, which poked out slightly through his closed lips, observed the work of his sinewy hands as they skillfully applied a fresh bandage to her tail. If she was to stay with him for any length of time, she needed to return the kindness and at least *try* interacting with him beyond a handful of responses. A few remarks and questions probably wouldn't hurt. If anything, it could offer further insight on how much she could trust him.

Capri cleared her throat. "I, um, never thanked you for finding me and rescuing me earlier today. I…don't know if I would have survived otherwise."

"Sure. I'm glad to have helped. I don't know what prompted me to check out the tide pools. Instinct, maybe? I'm just glad you're alright." Eden kept his eyes on his work, but decided to attempt some form of small talk and ask some lighter, easier questions since she was more responsive. "So, how do you speak my language?"

"The sea hears all," she answered. "It listens to the languages of those who have sailed upon it. I can't explain exactly how merfolk come to learn these languages other than the sea somehow passing that knowledge to us. I think we simply…*know* them as we age."

"How old *are* you, Capri?"

"I'll be thirty-seven solstices this summer."

His wrapping stalled as he tried to comprehend her meaning. "Wait, you track your age by solstice?"

"How do humans measure theirs?"

"By year. So, um, I guess by the passing of two whole solstices." He muttered softly while counting off his fingers. "That would put you around eighteen and a half in human years." *Ah, so I* did *guess right.*

"Is that young or old?"

"It's young, but humans might argue it's one of the best ages to be."

"What about you?"

Eden counted on his fingers again. "I guess in terms of solstices, that would put me at…forty-four solstices."

Capri arched her eyebrows in interest. "Are you considered young?"

"Old enough to be responsible and live on my own, but young enough to still have fun."

Capri nodded, feeling slightly less estranged now. For once, it was nice being around someone closer to her age. "I'm still considered young for my species, but regarded with many of the basic responsibilities of an adult."

"That's pretty much how humans operate. The independence comes with time. Speaking of which, if you don't mind my asking, are there other merfolk out there who might be looking for you?"

Capri waited until he had tied off her bandage before answering, "No."

Her tone was enough for Eden to drop the subject for now. "All done. Can I help you back into the pool?"

She tried lifting her tail herself, but not without straining. He slipped his hands beneath it. They were a welcome relief of support against the pain of the laceration. She allowed herself to relax into his hands, nodding her approval for his assistance.

"Alright, easy now," he said, angling her tail toward the water and setting it into the pool with the gentleness of a skilled marine veterinarian. He was so tactful in handling her, she almost couldn't feel his hands pull away. "How's that?"

"Good," she said. The tiniest smile flickered across her face before she slipped noiselessly into the soft glow of the pool. She felt lighter after her exchange with him. Perhaps her stay wouldn't be as scary as she'd anticipated.

Unbelievable, Eden thought, watching her resurface. *I have an actual* mermaid *in my own pool.* He still had so many questions, but he was willing to earn Capri's trust in due time. For all he knew, that time might come sooner than he thought, given their latest interaction.

As a courtesy, Eden shut off the lights to the pool for the night, but Capri insisted that he keep the other garden lights on.

"I want to sleep with the stars this close to the water. At least, that's what these lights remind me of."

"However you like it," he said, happy to oblige as her host. He wanted her to enjoy her time here, however long or short it might be.

Not too *short, I hope,* he thought. *Who knows how long it takes mermaids to heal?*

CHAPTER 4

CAPRI'S TRAGEDY

The memories of yesterday rushed into Eden's first moments of consciousness as the morning light peeked through his window. He was quick to throw on fresh clothes and a sweater before heading to the courtyard to check on Capri. He peered through the window to find her seated on the underwater ledge closest to the door, reclining against the pool's edge, nibbling on the kelp leaves he'd fetched her yesterday. She looked so content, he almost didn't want to disturb her.

Eden took the time to cook himself an omelet and brew a cup of coffee before heading out to see her. He peered outside the window one more time to confirm she was still by the poolside before jostling and turning the doorknob just loudly enough to alert her of his arrival. She didn't rush away like he imagined she might when he opened the door. Instead, she continued nibbling on a leaf, observing him intently as he descended the steps with his breakfast in hand.

"Good morning, Capri," he said.

She acknowledged him with a nod while chewing.

"I hope the pool worked decently for you. Did you sleep well?"

Her lips curved into a definite smile, wider than last night, at the memory of the lights. "I did. Your garden is a strange little paradise."

He stood a little taller at the remark. It was nice having his handiwork admired. "How's the tail?"

With a twinge of discomfort, Capri lifted her tail until the lower half poked out of the water, showing off the wound. "Better, actually."

He pulled up a chair to sit by the pool's edge. She had already removed the bandage herself, and by the look of it, he guessed she might not need it beyond one more binding. The wound was healing at a remarkable rate. No obvious signs of infection.

"I'll get a fresh bandage on it here shortly, but by tonight you may not need it anymore," he said.

"Huh. What's that?" Capri asked, craning her neck to see what was on his plate.

"It's my breakfast. An omelet." He lowered his plate to show her.

The food had a pleasant smell, but she narrowed her eyes as if doing so would help her decipher its makeup.

"That looks too complicated. Human food looks nothing like mer food."

"Humans can and do eat seafood, I promise," said Eden.

"How do they eat seafood if they're not merfolk?"

"Well, think about it," he said after taking a sip of his coffee. "Other sea creatures eat the same food as you, and *they* aren't merfolk. I don't think food necessarily determines the kind of creature you are."

Capri bit off a corner of kelp as she thought on his words. At this point, Eden expected long pauses between his remarks and her eventual response, so he proceeded to eat his breakfast in silence with her.

After he'd finished his last sip of coffee, Eden rose. "Speaking of food, I can go fetch you a fresh supply of food this morning and leave it here with you before I head out for the day. I'm going to need to follow up on the shark sighting with the other lifeguards. You'll be alright here on your own. You probably want some peace and quiet anyway."

"Okay," she said. Some space to herself sounded like a good way to acclimate to her temporary home without the constant presence of a human.

Once the dishes were washed, Eden headed out to the beach in his truck, bringing along a bucket this time to collect some oysters along with a fresh stalk of kelp.

Upon his return home, he presented them to Capri. "Hopefully, you can eat oysters."

She sat up a little. "Yes, I like those. But I don't have anything to open them."

A logistic he hadn't considered. "Wait! I've got it. I'll be right back."

He set the bucket down at the corner of the pool where they'd shared breakfast and dashed to his truck. He returned carrying the strange black metal bar she'd seen on the drive yesterday.

"What is that?" she asked. "I've seen those in the water on a few occasions. I could never tell what it was."

"This," he said, flicking open the blade, "is a pocket knife."

Her eyes went wide with intrigue. "They *open*? I never knew they could flip open. May I?"

Eden hesitated. "I mean, you can. But I have to warn you, it's sharp."

She settled onto the pool ledge. "Show me how it works."

Eden modeled the safe handling of the release switch and guided the blade to its open and closed positions a couple of times before handing it over to the mermaid.

"It's stuck," she said, struggling with the switch.

"Ah, it's more of a push than a sliding motion. I can show you."

When he placed his hand around hers, the whisper of a fuzzy tingle shivered down his spine. She was so soft. The heavy thickness of the knife emphasized the delicate silkiness of her scaled hands. He'd touched her plenty of times before. How was this any different? Blinking away the tingle, he guided her thumb to the switch.

"There you go," he said brightly. "Just beware of the blade when you open and close it."

He supervised her as she experimented with opening and closing the knife on her own. Her studious exploration was as dexterous as it was reverent.

"Not bad," he said. "This is the tool that we'll use to pry open the oysters. I can open them for you, unless you feel comfortable with the knife."

"You do it," she said, handing the blade back to him. "I'll learn by watching."

Eden proceeded to pry open the six or so oysters and laid them out for her. Her smile widened into amazement at the ease with which he opened them and the sight of sweet, fresh oysters made her mouth water.

"You're very kind," she said. "Thank you."

"It was nothing. Let's get a fresh bandage on you before I head out. Will you be okay while I'm gone?"

The mermaid nodded, much less anxious than she had been the last time he'd had to leave.

So far, so good, he thought.

The mermaid haunted Eden's thoughts all morning and into the afternoon. The whole situation was right out of the pages of a fairy tale. He wasn't altogether sure of how he felt about it yet. Certainly, hosting guests came naturally to him. He was known for hosting small gatherings in his courtyard or even having a friend crash on his couch for the night once in a long while. There was a certain thrill of having people over in a space that he could craft into an experience.

This time was different. He'd never had a complete stranger stay overnight, much less a girl, much less in his pool! The idea that Capri could still develop an infection worried him. What would he do then? Would he have to find a way to obtain antibiotics for humans or for marine life? If so, what type of sea creature? What if the medication didn't work? Or what if it made things worse?

I'd never forgive myself if she died on my account, he thought to himself. *It would be the only thing worse than when I—ack! Nope. No need to go there. Stop overthinking it. Take it one day at a time. What if* nothing *happens?* He resolved that if her condition deteriorated further, only then would he permit himself such anxieties.

Still, he was glad when the afternoon arrived, and he was dismissed for the day.

"I'm back! How was your day, Capri?" said Eden as he arrived home. *Huh, is this what it feels like to live with a wife?* He banished the thought before anything weird could germinate in his head.

"Good," said Capri, reclining comfortably on the underwater ledge. "I finished the oysters. They were delicious. I left the shells in the bucket for you."

Her cleanliness pleasantly surprised him. He had fully expected to find shells littering the pool floor. *That's better than most of my party guests.*

"There was also an extra oyster lost at the bottom of the bucket," she said. "You left the knife here, so I opened it like you showed me and pried open the last oyster by myself. It wasn't as scary as I thought it might be."

"Hey! Look at you taking charge." The pride on her face almost glowed. "And how's the tail doing?"

"It's hurting less now." She pushed herself up out of the pool and let him remove the dressing. She admired his gentleness as he ran his fingers on either side of the laceration. Not even her own species had regarded her with such reverence over an injury. She felt…important. Like she mattered. Like she was someone worth caring for. She should have resented how disarming a human could be, but like last night, she was finding this new experience refreshing.

"It's congealed nicely," said Eden. "No dizziness or feeling hot or ill?"

"Not at all. I could even swim more than yesterday."

"You're *sounding* perkier today too," he said. "Glad you're doing better. I think you'll be fine without a bandage from here on out. I've brought you some more food for this evening. More oysters and kelp. Let me go bring it in."

Eden delivered a fresh bucket of seafood for her and then went inside to make his own dinner, bringing it out to join her at the pool's edge where she was deftly prying open oysters.

"I learned more about the shark sighting today," said Eden. "It was a one-off sighting, and no one else on our team saw anything today. It's a little early for sharks to be showing up, but not altogether uncommon. Some hypothesize that the shark may have been drawn toward the shallows by another creature who had been injured."

"That was almost certainly my fault," said Capri.

"Well, now, I wasn't going to call you out on that. And I wouldn't call it your fault, per se. It was a cause-and-effect kind of situation. A colossal squid injured you, and then your injury attracted a shark. You couldn't help any of that, could you?"

Capri was quiet. "I—I think I could have."

Eden shook his head. "What do you mean?"

Capri tossed an empty oyster shell into the bucket, debating telling a human what had happened to her. Humans were the reason she'd fallen into this mess, and with an opportunity like this, she could spout every ounce of bitterness toward them. Oh, but Eden had been so kind, and it seemed wrong to tell him off when he had only done good to her. He'd given her many reasons to trust him. Even if he couldn't do anything to help her case, perhaps it would be good for her to impart her troubles to a human...if he was willing to listen.

"I love the coast, but I also vehemently despise it," she confessed. "It's a place I've always wanted to call home. I took every opportunity to explore the coast to watch the reflections of sunlight dancing on the water's surface, and watch the lights along the coast come on at night, sparkling like stars. I liked listening to the noises of the land traveling across the water. There were so many things I could hear even from far away, and it sounded like fun. Life always looked interesting on the coast, but like all merfolk, I avoided humans. They're such curious creatures."

"That we are," admitted Eden, rubbing the back of his neck. He'd never heard anyone describe the coast from the vantage of the sea. The way she described things felt akin to his lifelong fascination of the sea. "What changed your mind about the coast?"

"One time, I came close to the shore to explore, but there was a large vat of filth and refuse waiting there for me. Thankfully, I'd seen it before foolishly swimming through it, but it was devastating to see a coastal site reduced to a watery wasteland that neither human nor sea creature could inhabit. Even areas that I thought would be clear of debris were polluted. It would grow so thick at times, it would blot out the sunlight, killing off the wildlife."

Capri pressed her lips together, a line of pain wrinkling her brow. "After all of the laughing and joy I'd heard coming from the humans on the shores, I'd never have imagined they'd be so careless as to destroy something they supposedly loved. In time, I learned that humans are all the same. Every coastline is the same. It was on account of the humans that my people were forced to abandon their homes many times and retreat further out to sea, sometimes living in deeper places than we were used to."

Eden shifted in his chair uncomfortably, feeling a weight settle on his shoulders at her hurting. "Where are your folks now?"

"My pod and I were taken in by Antilles, one of the only deep-sea merfolk who took special pity on us as we sought safer waters."

"There are merfolk in *deeper* parts of the ocean?" said Eden, trying to mask his excitement.

"Yes," said Capri. "Deep-sea merfolk tend to keep to themselves and don't want to have much to do with those belonging to the sunlight zone. Even with some assistance, the deep isn't a safe place for a mermaid like myself. My brighter, shimmering scales are meant for shallower waters, so I always give away my presence by mere movement. I'm easy prey for deep-sea predators. I can hold my own though. My fellow merfolk have told me that I'm swift and agile. They must have been right because no matter how many times I've been chased by a deep-sea predator, I've never been caught. As far as I was concerned, dodging predators was better than dealing with the humans' pollution."

Eden wrinkled his face in remorse. "That sounds awful, Capri. Living like that? For how long?"

Capri shook her head. "Weeks, maybe? I lose track of time in the darkness. Even so, I'm the sole mermaid of my pod who has kept trying to visit the coast. A few others had joined me before, but with the increase of pollution, they discouraged me from visiting the coast. They've even berated me for visiting the shallows alone, saying it's too dangerous. That's why merfolk often travel in pairs for safety. I knew they might punish me if they caught me making a solo trip, especially with how young I am."

"But if you're treated like an adult, why would they punish you?"

"Forty or forty-two solstices is considered a more mature age in our species. Until then, merfolk like me are frequently treated with the protectiveness owed to a child."

"I get that," muttered Eden.

Capri sighed. "It's such a difficult age, and it didn't help with my longing to see the coast again. My heart grew sick for it. I was so desperate that I began to make occasional visits in secret, thinking that maybe this time, the pollution would be gone."

"I take it you were only disappointed with what you found," said Eden.

Capri rubbed her face and nodded. "When I think about it, maybe my elders were right. I was so stupid to ever believe in something as impossible as that."

"Oh, I wouldn't say that," said Eden. "It means you had hope."

She stared down at the long tear in her scales while fanning her tail in the water. "That hope only got me in trouble."

That didn't help. Eden laced his fingers together, locking away any further encouragements to avoid embarrassment.

"My luck ran out finally, yesterday afternoon," said Capri. "I suppose it was just a matter of time since the sea never created me for the deep. I'd just attempted another solo coastline visit, but I was disappointed yet again by another trail of pollution. This one extended for what must have been leagues. In a fit of rage to the point of what I can only imagine was madness, I dared myself to swim as far down into the depths as I could go. On the way down, I swam into something nearly invisible which ensnared my tail. It was a trap that I'd heard of before—a ghost net, left adrift by negligent humans. They've claimed many a mer's life, but I refused to be taken down by any human device. I tried to work myself free, but the more I yanked and dragged the net around, the more it entangled me. The net eventually snagged on the sea floor, and I began screaming, cursing humans for what they had done to me."

Capri's lower lip trembled as she replayed her explosive, feral cries in the lonely darkness of the deep. She had never known such fury and hopelessness. "I admit, I'd become too emotional to think. It was one stupid thing after another. Had I been even a little less enraged, I would have known better than to make such noises in the deep while trapped and at the mercy of predators. And what else would find me other than a colossal squid passing nearby?"

Recognition flashed across Eden's face. *So* this *was what she'd gone through before I found her*. Her dread was palpable as she recounted the scene.

"You've never experienced fear until you've crossed paths with a colossal squid. The instant I saw and heard it in the distance, my blood ran cold. It started as a silhouette growing larger and larger until I could identify its dreaded eye in the darkness. I frantically wrestled with the ghost net, but even as I tore my way out, it still pinned the end of my tail down to the sea floor. By the time the squid was nearly upon me, I could actually make out its arms and tentacles lined with spinning hooks. I've seen what happens to other sea creatures who are caught by those hooks, and I was not about to become one of them.

"I shouldn't have escaped. Maybe the ocean had a hand in it, but the squid's hooks snagged the net while I pulled it taut, tearing right through it. Finally free, I darted through its arms and tentacles, some of which became caught in the ghost net. The monster began to thrash, and one of its arms lashed about my tail, but I launched out of its grip before it tightened. I thought I'd beaten it, but as I rushed to the surface, I realized the creature had ripped a gash in my tail."

"Oh," breathed Eden. A shiver rippled across his skin as he eyed her injury with this new knowledge. He recalled that fear in her eyes when he'd found her in the tide pools, the likes of which he could see again as they welled with tears.

"I knew that the blood would attract predators," said Capri, "and the moment that I thought I saw a shark, instinct drove me to shore. I had no choice. I had to ascend through that thick nightmare of plastic and garbage. It clung to me like it wanted to drown me. I don't think merfolk can drown, but if they could, it would be like this."

Tears ran down the mermaid's cheeks. "I thought I was going to die, Eden. I really did."

A heavy silence hung in the garden, interrupted only by occasional sobs.

Eden shook his head, sad that there was very little he could do to mitigate her pain. "That all sounds so…terrible, Capri. I'm sorry you went through all of that. It sounds like it was very painful and scary. It's pretty clear to me, though, that the arrival of the shark was nature acting as it usually does. Like you said, I think you were following your instincts. Wounded sea creatures will do all kinds of things to escape predators like you did. We can't condemn nature. The shark wasn't your fault."

His mouth went dry as he fished for the right words. "I'm—sorry about the garbage. It never should have been there. I think it was reasonable for you to be angry for being let down by…human negligence. You should never have had to suffer like you did."

The sound of her breaths grew thin and shallow, stifled in her chest like a choked surf heavy with muck and litter.

"Hey there, remember to breathe," he said, coming down from his chair to sit by the pool's edge. "I'm here. You're here. And you're safe. There's nothing here that will hurt you."

The warmth of his voice was like the afternoon sun shafting through a thick ceiling of ocean refuse. It didn't solve the dread or remove the terror, but it offered hope from a place beyond the darkness.

"That's right, breathe," said Eden, hearing a shift. He inhaled a deep, regulating breath to guide her.

She closed her eyes as she took intentionally longer, deeper inhales. He could almost hear the ocean's rhythmic whisper through her lips, like when he'd first rescued her at the tide pools.

Then she did something that surprised him. As she found her rhythm once again, she rested the side of her head against his knee where he knelt beside the pool. The moment she touched him, he could feel an agitated ocean calming to a shimmering whisper inside his chest. He drew his hand to his chest. If only he could understand what this sensation was. He could only connect it to Capri, but couldn't explain anything beyond the association.

Capri eventually lifted her head and opened her eyes. "I feel a little better now."

The ocean in Eden's chest vanished as suddenly as it had manifested. "That's good to hear."

She dabbed away her tears. "Sorry, I've never told a human my fears before," she said through an embarrassed laugh.

Eden echoed her laugh. "I mean, have you *ever* spoken with a human before?"

"No." She chuckled. "No, you're my first."

He didn't know if it was her words or the sweet smile that broke across her lips when she'd said them, but a tiny swarm of butterflies fluttered in his stomach. He cleared his throat. "I'm—I'm happy to be an ear for you."

Capri gazed up at him with a sincerity and innocence that he would never forget. "I'm glad you found me, Eden."

"I—I'm glad I found you too."

The evening came and went with his usual gardening duties. Capri asked for the garden lights on the fence to be left on once again because of how they resembled the stars up close. Eden was glad to oblige.

As he shut off the lights inside to retire for the night, he stole one last curious glance through the window to see how his guest was doing after an emotionally tumultuous afternoon. It warmed his heart to see the mermaid floating peacefully on the pool's surface, staring up in wonder at the surrounding lights. Here she was, far away from all that had hurt her, immersed in the things that she'd long admired about the coast.

An idea came to him. He located a control panel next to the door which managed the lights in the courtyard. Feeling for the knobs by memory, he located the one that controlled a set of lights he had yet to introduce to his guest. He peered through the window as he turned the knob to the right. Along the slatted ceiling over the courtyard, strings of soft, warm fairy lights came to life.

Capri raised her head and straightened herself in the water. Eden grinned as her jaw dropped. Her open-mouthed amazement morphed into a smile as she spun slowly to take in the new light feature.

Eden glanced at the knob again. *Should I do it now or save it for tomorrow?* He shrugged. "Eh, why not?"

He twisted the knob to the right again.

Capri's amazement turned into electric excitement as the fairy lights began to twinkle softly. Her smile was so big, Eden couldn't help but wear one of his own. The pool was agitated with her excitement, and a laugh—an actual light, soft, cheery laugh—escaped from her lips, just loud enough to be heard through the window. The very sound made his insides tickle with a sensation of dozens of tiny bubbles fizzling with excitement.

Eden hugged his middle as he watched her. A working theory was forming in his mind: by some magic or unknown force, he was capable of feeling what Capri felt. Whenever she experienced a strong emotional shift, he could feel it somewhere inside of him through physical sensations that resembled the movements of the sea. Her desperation had felt like a longing surf against his rib cage, her return to relief like the calming of stormy seas, and her joy had quite literally felt bubbly. How and why he felt these sensations were questions for another day, but he went to bed that night feeling warmer and happier.

Chapter 5

Swimming with a Mermaid

Eden made his way out to the courtyard with his coffee in hand, which he drank more for taste than out of need this morning. A hum of excitement ran through him as he joined Capri in her usual spot on the underwater ledge, reclined and already eating her breakfast of oysters and kelp leaves.

"How was your night?" he asked, doing his best to suppress his knowing smile.

"Oh, Eden! It was absolutely magical," said Capri. "I was floating in the pool, and then out of nowhere, these beautiful tiny stars appeared overhead. And then, they started to twinkle! Like, actually sparkle like the real thing."

"Oh, really now?" said Eden, pulling up his chair.

"I'm serious! I've never seen anything like it. Well, maybe firefly shrimp and bioluminescent algae, but even they are nothing like what I saw last night. I thought I'd never sleep." Her smile widened enough to flash her pearl-like teeth. My, did they bring her smile to life!

"It sounds like it was quite a night," he said.

A smirk took the place of her grin as she eyed him sideways. "Did *you* have anything to do with those lights?"

"Oh, well, I, um, I may have known where a certain knob was that would turn on such lights—"

She smacked the water. "I *knew* it. I knew you must have been behind it."

Eden rubbed the back of his neck modestly. "I, uh, yeah. I thought you might like that."

"It was beautiful." She beamed. "Thank you for that."

Eden raised his coffee mug. "My pleasure."

Her demeanor was glowing today more than ever before. After another warm sip, he inquired about her tail.

"No pain since yesterday evening." She lifted her tail out of the water with greater ease than the last time, raising it so that her entire fluke flipped impressively out of the water.

"Very good," he said approvingly. "Not a trace of infection. You're a hearty mermaid."

"Well, that's what scales are for. They're a kind of thin, flexible armor plating designed to protect our skin from most scratches and injuries. Speaking of which, there's something I've been meaning to ask you."

Eden swallowed a flutter of anxiety down with his sip of coffee. "Ask away," he said as confidently as he could.

"What's it like having no scales on your skin?"

"Huh?"

"No scales on your skin," she repeated. "Does it hurt?"

"Um, no, not really. Well, I mean, it can. I guess it just depends."

"That's not very helpful. How can it 'depend'? Merfolk skin is covered by scales and is either protected from injury or sliced through. There is no in-between. And then I look at you humans." Her eyes scanned him up and down. "You're all fleshy and naked. I'm just confused as to how you function without scales for protection."

"I see," said Eden, thinking through his answer while finishing his coffee. "Well, our skin is strong enough for the world we live in. It moves in harmony with the changes and impacts of the world on our bodies. Your skin is designed for your world. Humans can get hurt on land just as much as you can get hurt in the sea, but we don't have the same kinds of dangers here as you do in the sea." He could almost see the thoughts settling in her head. "Skin doesn't necessarily determine all of our vulnerabilities."

Capri nodded. "I wonder how unscaled skin would behave in the sea."

Eden didn't bother mentioning to her that traditional depictions of mermaids usually involved bare-skinned, unscaled top halves. Besides, her fully clad scaling made her look far more dressed up than any half-naked mermaid.

"Can humans swim?" she asked finally.

"I have a pool, don't I?" said Eden.

"Oh, right. Silly question. I guess I'm asking because I don't understand how humans could possibly swim without fins or a tail."

"It's…different," said Eden. "We're land creatures, so there are many methods of swimming. Like this, for instance." He proceeded to demonstrate a classic breaststroke motion. "We use our arms to pull ourselves through the water, and we kick with our legs, kind of like this." He held onto his chair, leaning back as he proceeded to kick awkwardly with his feet in the air like a frog.

As if humans couldn't look any more ridiculous! thought Capri, and she actually laughed. A bright, loud, happy laugh from deep in her gut.

It was a laugh that filled Eden's torso with a sudden swarm of bubbles after a leaping splash into the water. The sensation was so much louder than last night that he sat up sharply.

"You could just *show* me," said Capri, gesturing to the pool.

Eden raised his brow. "Oh, you mean…"

"Of course. It's your pool anyway."

"Okay," he said, trying to keep his voice steady. He was already wearing his swimming trunks for work later that morning, so he had no excuse to delay his demonstration. He removed his jacket and his shirt, leaving them in a pile on the chair.

The mermaid's anticipation vibrated through the courtyard as he plodded over to the corner opposite her, dipping one leg after the other into the cool water to stand on the sunken ledge. He cast her a glance, but she didn't seem the least bit apprehensive. Exhaling, he finally sat himself down on the ledge.

A twinkle of excitement sparkled in Capri's eyes as she sat up taller. "Show me. Show me how humans swim."

He was a lifeguard. He knew full well how to swim, but his arms were like wet noodles. Why did he suddenly feel as nervous and self-conscious as he had before his first swim meet? Was it because he was shirtless in front of a pretty girl he'd only just met? Or the simultaneous thrill and fear of sharing the same water space with a mermaid? Maybe a combination of the two? Whatever the cause, his heart was pounding like he had already swum twenty laps.

It's just a swim, he thought to himself.

He took a deep breath and launched himself from the side of the pool. He let his mind go back to his old morning swimming routine, first demonstrating a butterfly stroke across the pool. Then he returned with a back stroke, stopping exactly where he always knew the ledge appeared before flipping seamlessly into a breaststroke for his third trip. He completed his final pass across the pool with a freestyle stroke that sliced cleanly through the water.

As Eden caught his breath at the edge of the pool, shaking water from his dark hair, Capri appeared beside him, startling him.

"That was unreal," she said, staring at him in wide-eyed wonder.

"Oh, uh, thanks, I guess," he panted, combing some longer strands from his face. "I used to start my mornings with a good swim here."

"I see. Fascinating that you don't have fins, and yet you cut through the water with ease. Especially that first way of swimming at the beginning. Your form was so familiar, I could have sworn that you were a merman disguised as a human."

"Oh, really now?"

"Yes! I didn't see you spreading your fingers much." She took his hand to examine it closer. "See that subtle fleshy webbing between your fingers?"

"Uh, yeah. All humans have that."

"Maybe, but it's an innate design to help merfolk swim. I have it too, see?" She froze as she realized that she was pressing her scaly palm against his fleshy one. Had she grown so comfortable with him already that she had started to trust him? She never could have imagined doing such a thing with a human. She slipped her hand back into the water as if to make herself forget what had just happened. "You…you swim well for a human."

"I-I've had a lot of practice," said Eden, rubbing the back of his neck and feeling it grow hot. "Uh, h-how do mermaids swim?"

"Why don't I show you?" she said. She dipped head-first into the water, and her tail followed with a splash.

Eden took the solitary moment to recollect himself. "Come on, get a grip, man. She's just a mermaid," he muttered. It felt strange occupying a space that was normally his, but had turned into hers. When he slid off the ledge to dip into the water, his anxiety was replaced with instant wonder.

Capri's body undulated much like a dolphin kick, but with such finesse and effortless beauty, he barely dared to blink. Despite the blurry limitations of his underwater vision, every detail about her was unmistakable in the glassy water. Whenever she swam facing the bottom of the pool, her aqua hair trailed behind her in long, perfect tendrils. Then she corkscrewed to face the surface, all without a moment's falter as her body continued to ripple with fluid movements.

Does she look this happy in the ocean? Eden wondered.

Her undulations turned into slow, delicate twists and twirls, as much as her wounded tail would allow. Though this wasn't the spacious ocean, she utilized every corner of the pool with a zeal he hadn't seen in her before. Whatever spell of dreariness she had been under upon her arrival, it had now been decisively broken.

She interrupted his thoughts by catching his hands and pulling him along, swimming beneath him with the biggest smile spread across her lips. Seeing her this close in action was like living in another reality. The feeling reminded him of when he had gone on a guided swim with dolphins, holding onto their fins and being carried a short distance. This moment, however, surpassed that wonder tenfold.

Capri ended their trip around the pool on the side of the underwater ledge where Eden sat himself once again to catch his breath.

"That was so much fun. Even my tail could handle it better," said Capri, slapping her tail fluke behind her.

"It's like I said—you recover quickly," said Eden, wiping the water from his face. "You looked very happy, Capri."

"You seem at home in the water too. I guess humans and merfolk can be a lot alike. You can hold your breath for a long time too."

"Do *you* hold your breath when you swim? I, uh, wasn't sure how that worked."

She gave him an incredulous look. "No, it's the same as breathing the air. I don't know how to explain it. I just… breathe."

"So, you don't have any gills?" he asked, eyeing her neck and ribs.

"No, I'm not *all* fish." She grinned. It softened to an expression more akin to curiosity and maybe even a hint of embarrassment as she lowered her voice. "I, uh, did have another question if you don't mind me asking."

"Yeah? What's that?" said Eden. He froze, forgetting to breathe when her hand rested against his stomach and she leaned toward him.

Wait, what is she doing? he thought, instinctively leaning away. *Is she trying to...kiss me?*

"Capri, what—?"

"What's this hole in your middle?" she asked, nearly in a whisper.

Eden followed her gaze down to where her curious hand was planted against him, her thumb brushing across his navel.

"Oh, that?" He exhaled, trying to hide his relief.

"I didn't want to be rude. It was impossible not to notice it when you took your shirt off. I hope it isn't a bad thing."

"Uh, no. No, it isn't." Although it hadn't been the kiss he'd dreaded it would be, he pulled himself up onto the edge of the pool to create some space. "This is called a belly button, or navel. It's...how do I say this? It's a sign of being a mammal, something we get from birth."

Capri chuckled, reclining herself on the underwater ledge as she had before. "Humans are so funny-looking."

Eden could guess why she'd been so curious because as he stole a glance at her own stomach, he could see that it was perfectly smooth. Her scales were like a form-fitting gown so he'd never thought to question the absence of a navel, let alone *notice* its absence.

"Merfolk are born from eggs like fish," said Capri, amused by his surprise.

"Oh," he said. He must have been staring longer than he thought.

"Despite our half-humanoid appearance, we aren't mammals. Huh, who knows? Maybe *we're* the funny-looking ones."

"Yeah, makes sense," he said. Still a little freaked out over what he'd mistaken as an act of seduction, he went to grab a towel from a bin near the house and started to dry himself off. He kept his back turned, in part to avoid Capri's curious stares, but also to obscure his face, which he was sure was flushing.

She's not her, man. She's not her.

"I had a really great time swimming with you this morning."

He turned to see the mermaid resting her head on her arm, red lips curving into a smile.

"I did too," he said. Admittedly, it had been refreshing to taste the water again. Even thinking about it had begun to calm his pulse.

"You said you used to swim every morning," said Capri. "Do you think you…might want to start doing that again?"

A half-smile crept across his face. "Yeah, I—I think I'd like that."

The blood in his face drained as instantly as it had colored it when a knock sounded on the gate. He whirled to face it, his veins running cold at the shadow peeking from beneath it where a pair of feet stood. *I wasn't expecting anyone!*

"What's that sound?" Capri's question felt as loud as a safety whistle.

"Shhh," he whispered, encouraging her back into the water with frantic pats to the shoulder. "Stay under until I come and get you. Whatever happens, don't be seen."

Capri didn't understand what was happening, but the urgency in his voice convinced her to do as she was told. She dove beneath the surface, keeping to the center of the pool.

Eden tried to signal for her to stay pressed against the deep side nearest to the gate where she was less likely to be spotted, but the agitated water made it difficult for her to make out his hand signals. Or maybe she didn't understand him at all.

Another knock on the gate. Louder this time.

"I'm coming," Eden called, draping the towel over his shoulders. People's faces raced through his head. He couldn't fathom who it might be. *Act natural,* he thought. *It's my home, my rules*. Steeling his fingers, he opened the metal latch and pulled the door open a crack.

"Eden! I hope I'm not interrupting anything." A portly older man stood on the other side with a bushy white beard and a wardrobe fit for a day on the California beachfront.

"Oh, Mr. Cuthbert. Back already?" said Eden, restraining a sigh of relief. He opened the door wider for his next-door neighbor.

"Yeah, my wife started coming down with something, and we figured it'd be best to just come home early from visiting the grandkids. Don't you worry. I didn't catch anything. We drove in late last night. I saw your truck in the driveway this morning and thought I'd pop by to pick up our mail."

"Oh, yes. Of course. Th-the mail," said Eden, drumming his fingers on his leg. "Yes. Right. I'll go get it." He turned on his heel and made for the house.

"Oh, no worries, son. No need to rush."

Eden grimaced as he heard the gate close behind Mr. Cuthbert's voice. He'd stepped into the courtyard after him like he usually did. Under normal circumstances, Eden would have welcomed his surprise visit and even offered him a cup of coffee. Asking him to wait at the gate was more likely to raise suspicion. Mr. Cuthbert wasn't nosy by any means, but he also wasn't one to miss details either.

"Ah, I do have to head out for work here in a bit," said Eden as he reached the door. "Just have a seat, and I'll bring the mail."

He made a beeline for the living room shelf where the mail sat. The envelopes flaked out of their once organized pile, and he fumbled to catch them as they smacked the floor. *Come on, faster!* He shuffled them into a vaguely squared pile as made for the door in a hurry.

"I've got your mail," he called out louder than was necessary. His heart sank into his stomach as he stepped outside.

Mr. Cuthbert was at the corner of the pool nearest to the house, staring into the bucket of roped kelp leaves in it. Beyond his shoulder, still hiding in the center of the pool, was Capri, and she was becoming more clearly visible as the water stilled with her lack of movement. Had he seen her yet?

"Mmm? Oh, yes. Thank you, Eden," said Mr. Cuthbert.

Eden's jaw clenched as he handed over the mail. As Mr. Cuthbert examined one piece of mail, Eden tried jerking his head slightly to signal for Capri to move to a different position. He could just see her staring back tentatively, but he doubted subtle movements could be seen from that angle in the water.

"I don't mean to pry, but what's with the kelp bucket here?" Mr. Cuthbert chuckled. "Trying to propagate some new plants for your garden, maybe?"

"Oh, that. It's…eh, just an experiment. Nothing important." He guided his neighbor to face away from the pool as he circled him back to the gate.

"Oh, now don't be so modest," said Mr. Cuthbert. "You put a lot of work into this place. There's always something new to look at. But if somehow you're able to get kelp to grow in your pool, let me know."

Eden grew dizzy with anxiety as Mr. Cuthbert threw a glance at the pool. The water rippled somewhat, but Capri was no longer visible. The vice of his jaw released. She'd moved.

"Oh, don't you worry, Mr. Cuthbert. You'll be the first to know," he said, keeping his guiding arm around his shoulder until he'd unlatched the gate.

"I'll hold you to that," said Mr. Cuthbert, pointing an expectant finger at him. "You're a talented young man, a lot of potential. With a little charm, you'll be catching a fine young lady with that big heart of yours." He poked him jovially in the chest.

"Aw, that's nice of you, Mr. Cuthbert."

Mr. Cuthbert's eyes creased with his bushy smile. "You're a good man, Eden. Don't ever forget that. My wife and I are always grateful for your willingness to watch our house and collect our mail while we're out." It was as if his speech had slowed to a frustrating drawl the closer he was to the gate, and it took Eden everything he had to not push the well-meaning man out of the courtyard and slam the gate shut.

"Always happy to help," said Eden. "Say hi to Mrs. Cuthbert for me, and I hope she feels better."

"I sure will. You take care now."

The gate clicked shut. Eden's legs felt like jelly as he sighed in relief. He wandered over to the pool where Capri was curled up in a tight ball in the corner on the deep end, her face buried in her arms. Not wanting to speak her name too loudly, Eden threw off the towel and slipped into the pool. She heard his splash and lifted her head to see him extending a hand to her.

"You okay?" asked Eden as they surfaced. "Did he see you?"

"Hard to say, but I don't think so," she said. "I think he went right past me and stopped at the corner where I like to sit."

"Yeah, he saw the bucket with the kelp."

"Did he ask about it?"

"I told him it was for an experiment. It qualifies as true because I'm experimenting with what kinds of foods I can find for you."

"Clever," said Capri. Satisfying the truth instead of outright lying was familiar to her people. "Who was he?"

"You know the neighbors I told you about who'd been out on vacation? They came home early, and I had been collecting their mail. Human stuff again. I'm so sorry, Capri. I didn't expect anyone would come by, and I should've made sure he didn't come in—"

"I understand," said Capri. "This is your home and your world after all. I really do like it here in your garden, but I—I don't belong here."

Those words twisted Eden's insides more than he cared to admit. "I know. I'll take you back to the ocean just as soon as you're well enough. You shouldn't have to hide constantly."

It occurred to him as he said this that even after she'd returned to the sea, her life might not be much different there with how much running and hiding she'd already been doing in the deep. It might be as difficult for her to stay here with him as it would be to return home. He could see it all in her eyes. Even worse, he could feel a strange, sad tug at his heart at the thought of saying goodbye.

"For now, this courtyard is yours, Capri," he said. "I promise, I'll do everything I can to keep it that way until I take you back to the sea."

"That Mr. Cuthbert is right." Capri beamed. "You *do* have a big heart. But how does having a big heart help you catch a lady?"

Eden pushed himself up out of the pool. "Hold that thought. I-I'm going to be late for work if I don't leave here soon."

"I'll see you this evening. Oh, and Eden? Thank you for taking care of me."

His smile was bittersweet. With his neighbors back in town, how long could he realistically manage to sustain that promise of keeping her safe and secret?

CHAPTER 6

HIDING IN SECRETS

Thankfully, keeping Capri a secret from the Cuthberts wasn't as difficult as Eden had expected. The foliage of the garden created a natural dampening effect, muffling the sound of their voices in the courtyard when speaking at a reasonable volume. Although the Cuthberts kept to themselves most of the time, there was always the chance of a surprise visit if they saw Eden's truck in the driveway. Usually, it was to bring over a baked treat or introduce a special new coffee roast that Mr. Cuthbert wanted Eden to try. In that regard, Eden hoped that Capri could return to the sea sooner than later to avoid such a risk.

Aside from the Cuthberts, Capri's stay was like its own secret vacation. Every morning before breakfast, Eden would come out to the pool to survey Capri's injuries, which improved twice as fast as a human injury. Then he would swim laps with her.

She always had a way of making each morning different. Sometimes she would swim right alongside him, trying to copy his stroke, and flubbing it terribly; other days she would swim beneath him, alternating between facing the floor of the pool and facing up to mirror him. She preferred the latter so that she could study his swimming style and attempt to imitate it later. Other times, as her tail continued to heal, she would dart all around the pool with the energy of a dolphin, leaping over Eden and twirling around him until he was surrounded by a cloud of bubbles. Whatever she did, her pure, innocent intrigue delighted Eden.

After the swim, which always felt too short, Eden would shower, cook breakfast, and eat with Capri. By the time 9 a.m. rolled around, he was out the door and off to work lifeguarding.

While she appreciated Eden's company, Capri rather enjoyed her alone time when he was out at work. It gave her the space to rest and regain her full strength, surrounded by the luxuriant garden of Eden, safe from the dangers of the sea.

In the earlier days of her stay, she felt homesick. Although she was thankful for the saltwater pool, she longed for the intense brine of the sea again. Her biggest consolation was the fresh seafood Eden would bring her. The flavors were a comfort in their own right. But her pod. Oh, how she missed the company of her pod.

What would my pod think of me now? she wondered sometimes. *Would they condemn me for accepting the help of a human? Probably. No, they would* have *to understand my circumstances, that I had no other choice if I wanted to survive. What was I to do otherwise?* She sighed at the thought of Eden's kind face and the way his gentle hands moved across her scales. She wouldn't have admitted it to herself, but a part of her looked forward to every small touch, however brief. It filled her with consolation and assurance that she would be okay.

"He's honest like a mer," she said aloud to herself one morning to cement her belief. "And he protects me like a podmate. He would *never* do anything to hurt me. I think…I trust him."

While he did his best to keep Capri safe from prying eyes, Eden ran into occasional trouble with keeping her a secret from his peers. His fellow lifeguards could be an inquisitive bunch, especially when he became quiet. They began their prodding barely six days after Capri had moved into the pool.

"Yo, Eden! You down for hosting a party this weekend?" asked Mike, one of the pushier lifeguards.

"Nah, I've got stuff to do," said Eden as he was wrapping up his shift.

"Since when did a single guy like you have 'stuff to do'? Unless…wait! You're not seeing someone, are you?"

"No, of course not," Eden retorted.

"Oh…it happened. It finally happened," said Mike as an impish grin pulled at one side of his mouth. "You hooked up with someone! Is she hot?"

"No!" said Eden sharply. Sweat beaded on his forehead. *Watch yourself.* "I mean, no, I'm not seeing anyone."

"I get it, I get it," said Mike, pretending to sound accommodating. "It's your first time with a girl—"

"Would you shut it?" said Eden, becoming testier while Mike was relishing his exasperation. "I'm not *seeing* anyone. Can't a guy just do his own thing for a weekend?"

"Alright, alright. You do you. But you've gotta at least attend the beach party this Friday."

"I'll…think about it. No promises though."

Mike snickered, muttering to himself, "Eden hooking up with a girl. Hah! Who knew he had it in him? I'd bet my entire paycheck it's Jess."

Eden snapped.

"You keep that name to yourself," he hissed, throwing his face into Mike's. He would have gladly seized him by the shirt if he hadn't been on duty. The muscles in his face twitched with a barely-contained rage as he spoke lowly but threateningly. "It's not Jess. It's not *anyone*. My personal life is none of your business."

Mike's grin didn't go away, but he backed away. "I get it. Still sour from the breakup."

"Jess and I were never a thing," said Eden through clenched teeth, nostrils flaring. "Now drop it before this turns into a formal harassment complaint."

Mike said nothing as he ambled off to his perch for his shift, but he was clearly satisfied with ruffling Eden's feathers.

Eden huffed as he climbed into his truck, slamming the door shut and re-slamming it when he wasn't satisfied with its aggression. He forked his fingers through his hair before resting his head in his hand. A queasiness roiled in his stomach as unpleasant memories flashed through his mind.

Laughter.

Hazy lights.

A drink in hand.

A girl unbuttoning his shirt…

"Jess," he hissed, almost gagging at the name as it slithered from his mouth. He didn't have the energy to think about her again.

He pounded the rim of the steering wheel before turning on the ignition. It was a temptation to peel out of the parking lot, but he kept his rage tight on his drive home, remembering to stop by the beach closest to his house to collect fresh oysters and kelp for Capri.

"Keep it all behind you," he told himself.

On occasion, when he arrived home, Eden would surprise Capri with some stray leaves of sea lettuce or a couple of wild shrimp in her bucket of food.

The best part of the day was in the evening when Eden cooked dinner and brought his plate outside to dine with

Capri while they talked and she pried open fresh oysters with the knife. Their chatter would continue as he tended to the garden, snipping stray vines and watering the hibiscus plants. He made a point to switch up his usual late afternoon solo workouts indoors in favor of a side-by-side workout with Capri. The more he swam with her, the more at ease he felt in her presence. Even his swimming techniques improved.

Although he would never admit it, even to himself, Eden was beginning to grow quite fond of Capri. Maybe it was an inevitability. Plenty of published lore often depicted mermaids and sirens as seductresses. Such literature, of course, was entirely fictitious, yet here he was with a mermaid in his pool. Some of the lore could be wrong. Maybe all of it. Anything was fair game at this point.

Even after the incident he had mistaken as a near-kiss, Eden had no reason to believe that Capri was any real threat. She had neither said nor done anything to tempt or enchant him. If anything, her innocence and curiosity had been the primary factors that had drawn him in. No other person had ever been so vulnerable with him or had placed their complete trust in him as she had. It fueled his sense of purpose.

She was also, admittedly, highly attractive. Whether she was in the water or sitting on the pool's edge, her two halves created an elegant S-curve that made her look as idyllic as the living, breathing subject of a painting. Sometimes, Eden would forget how far he had swum on a lap, almost crashing into the pool wall because he had been unable to take his eyes off of her lithe figure maneuvering gracefully in a liquid, rippling dance.

After their shared evening workouts in the pool, the swim would turn into a leisurely one. They would continue their chatter, keeping each other company into the late hours of the night if Eden didn't have work the next day.

Ten days after Capri's rescue, another loud, rather aggressive knock came rapping at the gate, this time during an evening workout. Capri didn't wait to be told to hide this time. She ducked under and hurried to the deepest corner of the pool, wincing as she scrunched her injured tail close to herself.

"Who is it?" called Eden as he approached the gate. Dread robbed his face of color at the silence that followed. Cautiously, he unlatched the gate and creaked it open a few inches at a time, craning his neck to peer around the door, revealing…no one. He stepped out to look around the gate, but no one was hiding there either.

Maybe a prank? "Hello? Is anyone—"

His foot knocked something over with a glassy clink. On the ground was an amber glass bottle of alcohol staring up at him. He picked it up, rotating it in his hands. There on the label, scrawled in messy black letters were two initials, *E + J*, with a sloppy heart inscribed around them.

"Mike," hissed Eden.

Capri ventured to the surface, daring a peek over the pool's edge as Eden re-entered the courtyard, closing the gate behind him. He was staring at the glass bottle in his hand, his jaw clenched. She was about to ask what had happened when Eden let out a startling yell, dashing the bottle violently into the concrete where it shattered, glass flying in all directions.

Eden immediately regretted his decision. He had foolishly broken glass next to a pool and was barefooted. He rolled his neck back, groaning as he rubbed the bridge of his nose. *I guess at least the glass is amber-colored,* he thought.

"Eden?" came Capri's trembling voice.

He turned to the pool to see a thin red streak on her face. *What have I done?*

"Capri! I'm so sorry." He hurried to the poolside to see a thin trickle of blood oozing down her cheek. "Are you alright? Ugh, I'm so stupid."

"I'm okay. Something flew at me…" Her expression shifted after she brushed her cheek with her hand and saw blood mingling with her scales. "Are *you* alright? What happened?"

Eden helped her out of the pool to better examine her face. "It's a long story. I did something stupid a long time ago, and it came back to haunt me today."

"What did you—?"

"I don't want to talk about it."

"Oh, okay," said Capri. She could feel remnants of rage dripping from his fingers as he surveyed the thin surface cut on her face. He grabbed his shirt from the chair and put pressure on the bleeding, which was already coming to a stop.

"Glass shard probably bit you in the face. Ugh! Why were you out of the water, Capri?" he said a little more harshly than he intended.

"I wanted to see what was going on." The crack in her voice fractured Eden's heart.

"Oh, Capri," he said, taking her face in his hands. She allowed him to press his forehead to hers. "I'm sorry. This was my fault. I shouldn't have done that. And now there's probably glass in the pool. I'll go down and clean it up before bed, I promise—"

"Eden," she said, grasping his wrist. She met his eyes. "You didn't mean it."

"What?" he said. He didn't know what he was seeing in her eyes. No one had ever looked at him like that.

"Someone must have hurt you. I can see it. You took it out on an object instead of a person. That was noble of you. It's a rare trait."

"But I lost my temper," said Eden, "and you paid the price for my impulsive rage. No, don't make excuses for me. I did something awful, and it hurt you."

Capri watched his face turn pale as he spoke. His hands began to slip from her face.

"Eden?" She caught him by the chest as he faltered, threatening to pass out. "Are you alright?"

She'd never seen him look so weak, and her reaction surprised even her. The longer she held contact with him in this vulnerable state, the more her prejudice against humans began to wane. *He's like us. Humans can become weak too.* Was she actually expressing real compassion for a *human*? She wouldn't have dreamed of such a thing ten days ago.

Eden steadied himself on his hands, but accepted her support as a wave of nausea rolled over him. "I'm… I'm fine. Just…a little dizzy."

"Eden, look at me," she said. When he didn't—or rather couldn't—turn his face, she reached for his chin, turning his ashen face to hers. "I'll be alright. I forgive you. But I still need you right now, so don't go passing out on me."

He managed a snicker at the last part. The life crept back into his head as he re-regulated his breathing.

"I'll even help bring you the glass pieces," she said.

"No, Capri, don't worry about—"

Too late. She'd already dived into the pool. Eden sat back, hand to his stomach as the nausea subsided. *I did something awful and she paid the price. This isn't the first time. So stupid! I'm no better now sober than I was when I—*

"I think I found all of them," said Capri, surfacing with three chunks of amber glass. They clinked as she set them at his feet. "I didn't see any more in the water."

Eden sighed, humbled by her cheerfulness at cleaning up his mess. "You're very sweet, Capri. If you're alright with sitting on land for a short while, I'll run the pool vacuum to make sure it's completely clear of glass."

She deserves everything I can give her, he thought. *I owe it to her now more than ever. She can never find out.*

Chapter 7

What is a Date?

Eden tried not to let the shattered glass event ruin the rest of his time with Capri. She was refreshingly cordial by not prying for more information after he'd refused to speak of his past. He couldn't stand pushy girls, so Capri was a breath of fresh air.

Every evening swim after the incident was a delight with Capri. She was always brimming with the strangest of questions: "How do plants grow on land? Why do reflections look different from underwater than they do just above the water's surface? How do humans walk? How do they breathe? If their bodies are mostly made of water, how do humans survive on land? Why do humans sweat? What is this 'aquarium' you've worked at? What do you do as a lifeguard? How do boats work? What are those long boards that make you stand on waves?"

Eden patiently answered all of her questions, at times stifling laughter at the innocence of her queries.

Something surprised him about their nightly discussions. As he imparted detailed explanations of common human practices to Capri, his eyes began to open to how much of his everyday life he took for granted. Small, thoughtless actions like walking, breathing, and even blinking began to feel important. Sacred. Magical.

Capri summed it all up one evening during a leisurely swim: "Being human sounds…beautifully and tragically wonderful."

"Yeah, I guess it kind of is," said Eden.

"What do you like most about being human?"

"Huh, I've never been asked that question before." He pondered his answer, but his pulse quickened at the thought of saying it out loud for fear of speaking it into existence.

"You can tell me," she encouraged, sensing his hesitation. "I won't tell a soul."

"All right, all right," said Eden, clearing his throat of as much anxiety as he could manage. He kept a thoughtful gaze up at the fairy lights to avoid eye contact. "The thing I like most about being human…is, well, something I haven't directly experienced before."

Confusion flashed across Capri's face. "You'll have to explain that one for me."

"It's difficult to put into words. It's something like... the ability to make a deep connection with someone, and they reciprocate that connection. It's deeply feeling the other person without the need for physical contact, hearing what the other has to say without ever having to speak, and knowing the architecture of their heart through a single touch."

"That's beautiful," said Capri after a long silence. "I'm not sure I understand how any of that works, but if I did, I'd like to think it *would* be the best part about being human. But how can you like that the most if you've never experienced it for yourself?"

"You don't have to have experienced something to know it's the best part of being alive," said Eden. "I know plenty of people who have lived out exactly what I described, and they're some of the happiest, most content people I know."

"Is there a word for it?"

Eden wavered his head back and forth. Spelling out what being in love was without explicitly saying it had been stressful enough. He wasn't sure he could say anything more without her asking questions that would make his nerves quiver.

"There are...a lot of words that could fit its meaning," said Eden. "I really couldn't begin to list them all."

She propped her elbow on the pool's edge. "Humans are so bizarre," she said, shaking her head but strangely enjoying the mystery of what it meant to be human.

Eden's gaze wandered over Capri's delicate facial features while she watched the hibiscus plants closing their blossoms for the night. *I know, I know,* he thought to himself. *I shouldn't be getting attached. But she's been the best part of the last two weeks. She's made me feel more alive than I've felt in a while. Oh, I wish I didn't have to take her back to the ocean tomorrow. Wait, how long has she been looking at me? How long have I been staring?*

"Something on your mind?" asked Capri.

Eden tried to play it cool. "I—I was just thinking…or rather, I was going to say…I'm going to miss having you around."

Capri gave him a sad smile. "I'm going to miss you too."

Butterflies filled Eden's stomach again. *She's a mermaid, and she needs to go home to her own kind.*

"I've had a lot of fun here," said Capri, playing with a strand of her hair. "I do miss the ocean, but if I'm honest, I wouldn't have minded extra recovery time to hang out here a while longer. I guess it couldn't last forever though. Tomorrow's the day, right? I do have one request for when you take me back. Um, remind me, you're not working tomorrow, are you?"

"No, not for the next three days," he said. What was he to do with himself after he'd returned her to the ocean?

"Okay then. If you're taking me back to the sea tomorrow, could you show me—oh, what was it called?—surfing."

Eden lit up. "What a great idea! I'd love to do that. It'd be a great last date together." *Did I just say* date? "I mean, last *day* together."

Capri grinned, acutely aware of his blunder based on his exasperated recovery, though she wasn't entirely sure of its meaning.

"Why don't we leave earlier in the day?" suggested Eden, trying to move on. "We can leave after breakfast, and I can take you to one of the quieter beaches nearby where no one will see you. I'll bring my surfboard and some food—well, I guess food for myself since you can eat what you like in the ocean—and I can show you what surfing is. I think there's some decent wind expected tomorrow, and, um...yeah, wh-what do you think?"

Capri's smiling eyes twinkled under the fairy lights. "I'd like that."

Ugh, that smile. She's killing me! Perhaps it was because this was their last night together, but she looked particularly beautiful tonight. The garden lights contoured the top of her head in a soft halo, and her hair was a thick, aqua curtain draping regally over her shoulders which glistened in the intimate lighting. And her sweet, soft, innocent face...

"Eden? Did you hear me?"

"Huh?" Eden snapped out of his thoughts, suddenly aware of her hand on his shoulder.

"You didn't hear me, did you?" she said sweetly.

He shook his head.

"I was asking if you were alright. Your face changed color."

Eden wanted to sink under the water to hide, not like that would do him any good with a mermaid. He splashed a handful of water on his face. "I-I'm fine," he said quickly. "It's just a human thing. I just… I-I think I was embarrassed is all."

"Embarrassed? About what?"

Eden's heart was pounding again at her touch. He casually ducked himself under the water to slip out of her hand. "Sorry, what was the question?" he asked as he resurfaced.

Capri giggled. "You're really nervous right now, aren't you?"

Eden forced a laugh, which came out sounding bewildered. "I, uh…k-kind of?" A strange feeling was forming in the pit of his stomach.

Capri took his hand. "Whatever for? You can tell me. Here, I'll help you out. I won't even look at you." She spun herself around, crossing her arms and turning her back to him, hair swishing about. "You're still nervous, I can tell. *You* turn around. No distractions." She listened as he turned to face away from her. "Alright now, I'll ask, you answer. What is a 'date'? You said the word when you meant 'day' just a minute ago, and it got you all flustered. Is there something special about a date?"

Eden cleared his throat, trying to thread his words together. "Um…a date. Well, a date is an…occasion where…

two people spend some...dedicated time together with the intent of...getting to know one another, often in a place that one or both of them have never been."

"Oh," chirped Capri, like something had clicked for her. "Like us right now?"

Eden's stomach flipped. "Ah, well, I wouldn't call *this* a date."

"Why not? We are two people, spending dedicated time together, we're getting to know each other, and *I'm* here in a place that I've never been—your pool."

Eden was lost for words. She wasn't wrong.

Her voice oscillated in his direction as she said, "So... it's a *date*. Right?"

When he allowed himself a glance over his shoulder, she was doing the same. How was every pose she struck that evening prettier than the last?

"I guess so," he replied, slowly accepting what she was saying, or rather, what he had accidentally defined between them.

"Dates are kind of fun. I like our dates," she said.

"I—I like them too," he said, fully facing her again.

"I *know* you do."

Eden knitted his brow. "You do? How?"

"Well, you're always smiling when we're together, even more so when you're in the water with me. It's funny, you'll stare at me like it's the first time you've ever seen a mermaid. Kind of like right now."

Eden's face grew hot.

Capri let out a chortle which devolved into a fit of laughter. The courtyard echoed with her bubbly laugh, threatening to disturb the neighbors at this late hour. The last thing Eden needed was prying eyes peering into his courtyard or knocks on his gate.

"Shhh!" he hissed, trying to cover her mouth. Thinking quickly, he seized her by the waist, pulling her under with him where her continued laughter wouldn't be audible.

Eden tried to shout her name, but it came out all garbled with air bubbles.

Capri slipped a polite hand over her mouth as she calmed herself. When she finally did speak, Eden was stunned by its bell-like clarity. Not a single air bubble had come out of her mouth as she'd laughed or even when she began to speak. "I'm sorry, it's just…your face changed color again. Did I embarrass you?" A rogue laugh erupted from her again. "I didn't mean to, I promise."

Already in need of air, Eden resurfaced, and Capri followed, stifling a soft laugh before she continued. "You've always seemed so sure of yourself, but tonight—well, I've never seen you act so nervous before. I think it's funny."

Eden forced a laugh to relieve his nerves, but it turned into an authentic laugh which he muffled with his hands, careful to avoid disturbing the Cuthberts. He had to admire her sense of humor. "Well, Capri," he said, sounding more like his usual self, "I guess you're right. I guess this technically *was* a date."

"With all the human terms you've been sharing with me, is there a human word or term for people when they are, uh, I guess the word would be dating?" asked Capri.

Eden didn't want to answer that. He'd intentionally left the romantic terminology of "boyfriend" and "girlfriend" out of his dating definition so as not to torture himself later after she was gone. She certainly wasn't helping.

"Let's, uh…let's call it a night," he said. "We can talk more tomorrow. Okay?"

Capri looked disappointed, but she accepted his call. *Should I tell him now?* she thought, watching him swim toward the end of the pool.

Eden was climbing up onto the underwater ledge when he heard Capri cry, "One more thing!"

He'd barely turned when the mermaid threw her arms around his torso. He stiffened and his breath escaped him, praying she couldn't hear his heart pounding as her head pressed against his bare chest.

"Thank you," she said. "Thank you for everything, Eden. I had fun on our date tonight. On *all* of our dates."

Eden found his breath again as she let him go. "I had fun, too."

A nameless warmth curled in his gut when she bunched up her shoulders, biting her lip mischievously as she replayed his embarrassed flushing in her mind.

"Okay, well, goodnight." She waved.

"Goodnight, Capri." He proceeded out of the pool and toweled off.

Capri watched as he collected his jacket from the lawn chair, tossing it over his naked shoulder as he made his way back into the house. A shiver rippled over her at the memory of his hands around her waist moments ago. He had never touched her like that before. It was different and strangely…pleasant. It made her feel warm and enlivened. Did this feeling have a name?

Yes, I'll tell him tomorrow, on our final date, she thought to herself. *Before we say our last goodbye—before sunset—I'll tell him.*

Once the door had closed behind him, Eden shut off the lights, dreading the lonely darkness that greeted him. If only it was as simple as that to shut off the feelings he'd been suppressing all evening. He fumbled to collect his jacket from his shoulder, but his fingers had lost their dexterity. No amount of willpower could persuade him to catch the garment as it slid to the floor. His head swam. When his legs threatened to buckle, he pressed his back against the door, hopelessly trying to hold back the ocean of longing for the mermaid on the other side of it. The more he resisted, the more the ache intensified in his chest.

"I can't say it. Don't say it," he whispered, wanting nothing more than to confess his…appreciation for her. No, his…*attraction* to her. Not that. Every word trickled through his head, but he refused to even think of the one he knew his heart was dying to say.

Swallowing, he peered out through the narrow gap in the curtain. There she was, as surreal as a dream, her healthy tail flitting in and out of the water. Such beautiful scales, too—as smooth as skin and as silky as the purest water. He could still feel the ghost of her arms wrapped around him and her face pressed against him. How he wished he could continue spending his nights with Capri, talking about the things that made life beautiful while drinking in every bit of her beauty. He would never bore of staring at her face, beautiful and mysterious as the island of her namesake, her cascading hair as pure as a waterfall, her eyes that sparkled like the sun on the water, and lips as mesmerizing as a sunset as they met with his—

No! What am I doing? I can't.

He clenched his hands into fists. Although he couldn't have been more grateful for his time with Capri, it had begun to feel ill-fated. As the minutes slipped away, he became painfully aware of all that could never be. Passion and grief entwined around his heart, threatening to rip it in two.

The strange feeling in the pit of his stomach had begun to intensify, writhing and swelling up into his chest, branching through the rest of his body. It was a longing; a restless, insatiable craving from the deepest part of his being. Resting his forehead against the door, he shut his eyes, heart pounding in his ears, and in a nearly inaudible whisper, the forbidden words he had been suppressing all evening slipped out before he even knew what he was saying.

"I think…I've fallen in love with Capri."

Chapter 8

The Best Day of Her Life

Eden ate his breakfast alone inside the next morning, though he could hardly taste it. It was no use torturing himself by spending any more time with the mermaid he'd fallen for than was absolutely necessary. It would make their parting less painful, even if by a small margin.

"Ready to go home?" asked Eden, pulling on his sweater. The early morning breeze was rather chilly. He didn't know how she managed so well in colder temperatures.

Capri looked distracted herself, like she'd been lost in thought. "Mhmm, I'm ready."

He detected a pinprick of sadness behind her oceanic eyes. Oh, those eyes. He was going to miss seeing them. "Great. Let me load up my surfboard and supplies for the day, and I'll come and get you last."

"Take your time. I wanted to say goodbye to your garden anyway."

The vice around Eden's heart clamped tighter. Why did this have to hurt so much? He very nearly dragged his feet as he made his trips back and forth to the truck, sometimes grabbing one item at a time in a feeble attempt to delay the inevitable.

It'll be a great time today, he tried to tell himself. *We'll have a lot of fun, I'm sure. I just have to keep my feelings in check.*

"Everything's loaded," he said, squatting by the poolside to meet Capri. He waited as she daintily kissed one of the red hibiscus blossoms, which matched her lips, a fond farewell.

That's one lucky flower, he mused.

When she had kissed every flower, Capri pushed herself up out of the water and onto the pool's edge, wringing out the excess water from her long hair. "I'm ready."

Eden proceeded to wrap one arm behind her back and tuck the other beneath her tail to pick her up. The task of carrying her had become wearisome, with the heaviness in his heart extending to his arms. His breath hitched when she tucked her own arm beneath his and wrapped it around his side in a trusting embrace.

"You alright?" she asked, resting her other hand on his chest with concern.

It was near impossible to answer. The words were caught wrestling with desire somewhere in his throat. "Yeah. Y-yeah, I'm fine. I—I'm just…"

"Excited about our last date? Me too. I can't wait to see surfing up close!"

The Cuthberts weren't home at that time, so Eden was able to carry the mermaid to the front seat without notice. This time she insisted on trying to buckle herself in. He was impressed by her memory because she figured it out almost immediately. He drove at a crawl more for himself than for Capri's sake.

After a couple of agonizing minutes, he pulled up to the wide shoulder of the road beside a metal railing, overlooking some sea cliffs.

"We're here," he said upon opening the passenger door.

"Can you unbuckle me, please? I forgot to pay attention to how you did it last time."

Eden wet his lips as he reached over her to unfasten the seatbelt. Maybe it was an electric energy sparking between them as he leaned close to her, or maybe it was his face starting to turn color again. Either way, he worked quickly.

"How are we going to get down there?" asked Capri, craning her neck. "It looks awfully steep."

"It is, but I can carry you. You're very light. Just hold on tight, and you'll be fine. Here, climb on," he said, turning his back to her.

"Okay. I trust you," she said.

She reached her arms over his shoulders and steadied herself against him. Eden stepped away from the truck until her tail dangled freely, her fins tickling his ankles. She was no lighter than a backpack.

"How's that?" he asked, helpless to slow his racing heart.

She shifted on his shoulders. "A little uncomfortable, but I think I can manage. Oh, wait! I have an idea."

Eden gasped at the sensation of her long, slippery tail wrapping around his waist.

"There, that's much better. Now I'm ready!" she said, resting her chin on his shoulder.

Eden silenced a gulp. *Feelings. In. Check.*

Eden had visited this secluded beach many times, so he had no trouble climbing down to the beach below. At least, not technically. As short of a descent as it was, it felt like ages to him with Capri clinging onto him. He could hardly focus.

Once at sea level, he lowered her in front of a smooth boulder, breathing a sigh of relief as she released her grip on him. Feeling sweaty, he slipped out of his jacket and stepped away to recollect himself, doubling over and bracing himself against his thighs like he'd just completed a sprint.

"Are you alright?" called Capri.

"Yeah, just…taking a break."

"I don't think I got *that* much heavier being away from the ocean."

Oh no! Did I just call her fat? Eden whirled to face her, eyes wide. "I-I didn't mean it like that," he cried apologetically. *Oh, now you're* really *screwing up this date.*

"I'm just kidding." She chortled. "Take all the time you need. The ocean is forever, but I only get Eden for a day."

The words were bittersweet to his ears, but also surprisingly encouraging. *She's right. She only gets me for a day, and she deserves the best version of me. Come on, man! Get out of your head and give her the time of her freaking life.*

With a new sense of determination, Eden righted himself, squared his shoulders, and strode back to where Capri was busily combing her fingers through the ends of her hair.

"Ugh, dry hair always gets so tangled up—woah!"

Her cry of surprise at being swept up into Eden's arms morphed into a sunny laugh as he started spinning her in circles. She extended one arm, cutting through the air like the breeze on a seagull's wings. If this was what flying felt like, she almost envied the birds.

"That was wild! What was that for?" She laughed, catching her breath from the excitement.

"You said it yourself. You only get one day with me, and I'm going to make it a day to remember."

Eden didn't think her smile could get any prettier, but it did. His heart leapt when she clasped his shoulder.

"You mean a *date* to remember," she corrected with a smirk.

Their final date began with Capri's reintroduction to the ocean. Eden held her close as he waded into the surf. When the water was up to his hips, he lowered the mermaid into the water.

A wave of ecstasy washed over Capri's face as the sea rushed over her scales. She very nearly broke out into tears of joy. The sea had never tasted so sweet. Then Eden almost imperceptibly slid his arms out from under her, allowing her to sink back beneath the whisper of the waves. Tendrils of her hair rose all around her. They mingled lovingly with the familiar particles of the sea. She reached behind her to find the sea floor, digging her fingers into the fine, cool sand. She closed her eyes, relishing the caress of untamed saltwater flooding over her scales.

After all this time, she was home.

Eden thought he would feel sad when he let Capri slip out of his arms. Instead, he felt a sudden calm. It was not unlike the feeling of being out in the open water on a tranquil day where nothing in the world could disturb his peace. Was this what Capri was feeling? It had to be. He stood motionless for a while, unable to see Capri beneath the foamy surf.

Maybe she's gone for a swim? he wondered. *I wouldn't blame her. I'd miss this place too if I were separated from it for too long.*

He waded back a few steps, looking out at the beautiful blue landscape. He called this home too. Sometimes he could hardly believe that he had the privilege of living here. All of those conversations with Capri, describing his views from the lifeguard chair to the tops of the sea cliffs—none of them compared to experiencing it firsthand.

A larger wave came rushing up, encouraging him to back toward the shallows, but he paused when he saw an unusual shape in it. As the wave broke, Capri sprung out of the white foam, tackling him into the shallows in a fierce embrace, burying her head in his chest.

"Thank you, Eden," she sobbed, seizing and twisting the fabric on the back of his tank top. "Thank you, thank you, thank you."

Eden propped himself up to sit, but she clung to him like her gratitude depended on it. "Hey it's alright—"

Then she kissed him. On the cheek. It was as sudden as it was real. Her lips were planted on his face just long enough for him to register what was happening. And then she withdrew, unmistakable tears welling up in her eyes.

Eden couldn't think. He couldn't move. He just stared at the mermaid, dumbfounded.

"I'm home, Eden. I'm *home*!" said Capri, barely able to keep her sobs at bay. "And it's all because of you."

In a daze, Eden brought a hand to his cheek, but stalled. The sensation of her lips on his skin lingered. They had pressed surprisingly close to his own lips, with perhaps a finger's breadth to spare. He didn't want the sensation to go away.

Instead, he reached up to Capri's face and brushed aside some wet strands of hair sticking to her cheek. His breath returned to him as he spoke, grateful that the noise of the surf hid the tremble in his voice.

"You *are* home. I was happy to help."

Capri buried her face in his chest again and squeezed him, sobbing like she'd never let him go. Eden sat up more and wrapped an arm around her, returning the embrace. The only other time anyone had ever wept in gratitude like this was when he'd helped a frightened child, lost and separated from her parents, and she'd hugged him, casting all of her trust on him. Capri's grip was not unlike that of the child's—trusting, vulnerable, grateful for having a young man who was strong enough to bear her burdens with her. He felt accomplished. Proud. Overflowing with love.

Then his pulse stumbled at an embarrassing realization—she was lying on top of him. As his face grew hot, he swiveled his head left, right, and over his shoulder to see if anyone was watching. It was already commonplace for his friends to give him a hard time about being single, especially his fellow lifeguards, who'd made a game of pointing out girls on the beach for him to date. The thought of being caught lying on a beach with a pretty girl—let alone a *mermaid*—draped on top of him chased away any hint of enjoyment of the tender moment he shared with Capri.

"Come on, now," he coaxed, turning himself over so that she slipped into the crook of his arm to gaze up happily at him. "The day is only so long, and I haven't shown you what surfing is yet. Would you still like to do that?"

Capri blinked away a happy tear. "This is going to be the best day ever."

The rest of the morning and afternoon offered grand ocean swells and a perfect wind. Eden retrieved his surf board and paddled out into the open water with Capri swimming alongside him. It had been a while since he'd done this, but as he paddled over the increasing swells, it all came back to him. It was like sitting on the ocean's chest as it rose and fell with a long, primal breath.

When it was just right, he would catch a wave. Capri would follow, riding alongside him. Other times, she would leap through them like she'd seen dolphins do to try to outrun Eden. Still other times she would watch him from beneath the wave as it arced and broke. She liked it whenever he touched the waves. She imagined the ocean must feel the same delight at his touch that she felt whenever he touched her scales.

The ocean must love him to allow him the pleasure of surfing on it, she thought. As she followed him on the inside of the wave while he cut through it, she reached out to meet his hand. He shot her a knowing smile. It was one that strangely made her heart flutter.

Every time Eden eventually toppled into the water, he could sense Capri coming close. Although he pretty much never opened his eyes underwater in the ocean, by the time he surfaced, he would seek out Capri's aqua tail glinting in the sunlight. She would always meet up with him after every wave.

She laughed after a particularly pristine wave. "That was unreal!"

"We lucked out today," he said. "These are the best waves I've ever ridden."

"It's like the ocean *wanted* you to have fun," she said.

"Well, I don't know about that—"

"No, I'm serious. I think the ocean was trying to say thank you for doing something kind for it."

Eden laughed uncomfortably. "Me? What did I do?"

"You rescued me. You helped me recover. And you brought me home." Capri looked out at some waves further out along the horizon. "The ocean rewards those who are kind to it, and I think it wanted to do that for you."

"Maybe. I mean, I think it was more of a 'welcome home' for you."

"You might be right. Honestly, I could never repay you for what you did for me." *Actually, there is that one thing...*

"Hey, why don't we head back toward the beach?" said Eden. "It's going to be evening before you know it. If you'd like, we could watch the sunset from this one sea cliff that offers excellent views."

Her eyes grew wide with excitement. "The sunset from a sea cliff?"

"Trust me, you've never experienced a sunset like the ones seen from atop a sea cliff."

"If you say so."

I'm running out of time, she thought. *I need to tell him. Okay, yes, I'll tell him while we watch the sunset. It's then, or I've lost my chance.*

CHAPTER 9

SUNSET ON THE SEA CLIFFS

As afternoon gave way to evening, Eden returned everything to the truck, then carried Capri back up the steep slope to the road. He was less anxious this time about having her cling to him. If anything, he kind of liked it, but it didn't make his heart pound any less. Something about her kiss that day had given him life. Energy. The feeling like he could run a marathon.

Once he had made it to street level, he followed the outside of the railing for a few dozen paces until he came upon a rocky protrusion—the top of the sea cliffs.

"Hold on, now," he said, turning to climb down a nearly vertical rock face. Every crevice was as familiar to him as home, which was a good thing because he might have otherwise fumbled his grip when Capri nervously tightened her arms and tail around him in her fear of falling. Every move she made was as pleasant as it was distracting.

In less than a minute, his foot met the flat of a cliffside ledge. It was large enough for three or even four people to sit upon comfortably, so he and the mermaid could both sit with just enough distance from the drop-off to extend both legs and tail.

"Well, what do you think?" said Eden.

Capri's slacked jaw became a wide smile filled with wonder. It was like seeing the ocean for the first time. The seascape before her sparkled with sunlight as it began its descent into the ocean. From this vantage point, the sea appeared as an indigo blanket, shifting about slower than at sea level, whispering its stories of the day. A handful of sailboats dotted the water, appearing more as weightless paper triangles rather than as heavy vessels of wood and fiberglass as she'd seen them below the surface.

Capri couldn't stop shaking her head in wonder. "It's prettier than it looks at sea level. How did you know of this place?"

"This is a secret spot I found in my high school years."

"Are you the only one who knows about it? Is it *your* secret?"

"Nah. See that?" he said, pointing at a wall-like section of rock behind them. A litany of letters appeared to be inscribed in the stone. Some letters were encircled by unusual shapes, a few of which had arrows pointing out of one side.

"What does all this mean?"

"Those are people's initials, the first letter of their name. These are people who've been here." *No point in explaining what a make-out spot is either,* he thought.

Capri ran a finger through some of the letters, tracing their foreign shapes. "So, is this like a human tradition?"

"Yeah, in a sense. Like you said, humans are weird."

She hovered over one of the sets of letters with a large curvy shape around it. "What makes these so special?"

He didn't want to lie to her, but he couldn't just say outright what it was. "Do you remember how I told you about the thing I like most about being a human?"

Capri nodded.

"Well, people who feel the same way have visited this place to etch their initials into the cliffside. Sometimes, they carve a heart shape around them as a universal symbol of that feeling."

"Oh! Where's yours then?"

Something between embarrassment and regret crossed his face. "I've never put mine up here."

"Is it because there has to be two people to do it? *I* could do it with you."

"Well, I don't know about—"

"What does the letter of my name look like?" she said, studying the wall as if she might crack the strange code on her own.

Eden knew there was little point in resisting. He found a loose, pointed rock and handed it to her.

"What's this for?"

Taking her hand which held the rock, he guided her to an empty space on the stone surface. Together, they traced the shape of a circle into the stone, stopping when it was two-thirds complete, creating a "C" shape.

"That's my initial?" said Capri.

"Mmhmm, the letter 'C' for Capri." Eden privately savored the feeling of her hand after he had released it.

"Can you show me your initial?" She handed over the rock.

"Alright, why not?" Eden took it from her and was about to carve a vertical line into the rock when Capri set her hand on his. His heart fluttered.

"I want to do it with you," she said. "I want to remember what your name feels like."

He disguised his heartache with a smile, then proceeded to guide their hands to an empty space beside the "C" in the wall, carving a series of four geometric lines.

"That's 'E' for Eden."

So that was what his name felt like. Capri released his hand, caressing the new lines with reverence like she was exploring a hidden piece of soul.

"Eden," she whispered.

Just as Eden thought to discreetly chuck the engraving rock over the cliff's edge, she picked it up.

"We forgot to add this symbol," she said, pointing to the pair of perpendicular lines between a neighboring set of initials.

Eden's stomach squirmed. "Uh…sure, go ahead."

The sound of permanence scraped against the stone cliff as Capri etched a plus symbol between the "E" and the "C."

"There! Now they're connected like all the others," she said.

"Yeah," he breathed. *At least she didn't ask to have a heart traced around our initials.*

A visceral sadness pulled like an anchor in his chest. The fresh engraving was a cleansing contrast to the one scrawled on the bottle label last week, but it still glared at him, reminding him of what he was about to lose—a pure soul, as alive and as real as the sea, a friend who had inspired a new love for life and had given him more purpose than he'd ever believed possible.

Satisfied with her work, Capri leaned her shoulder into him, resting her head against his chest. Eden swallowed, but he wrapped an arm around her back, holding her close. A smile spread across her lips as she relaxed into him, keeping her eyes on the water as the orange sun disappeared into the ocean, leaving a cascade of warm light beaming across the sky with the evening breeze. She had seen thousands of sunsets over the sea, but none had ever been quite this magical. Never in her life had she felt so content.

Eden kept his gaze on the ocean, but he was keenly aware of every surf-like breath and every move that Capri made. Her body sank into his just as gradually as the sun sank into the sea. A quiet peace engulfed them. For the next few minutes, nothing else in the world mattered.

The newly engraved letters nestled amongst the others stared at them. Eden flicked his eyes to them, imagining for the briefest of moments that what he and Capri had was as real as their initials declared on the wall that bridged the gap between land and sea. Was this really what having a girlfriend was like? Why had he run for so long? He did his best to lean into the blissful timelessness of this moment, but a looming dread crept in as the sky changed from golden orange toward a pinkish purple.

This is goodbye, isn't it? he thought. A lump knotted in his throat as he unconsciously hugged her shoulder a little tighter. He would miss every bit of her.

"I'm glad I met you, Eden," said Capri in her sweetest voice.

Eden tried to keep his voice from cracking. "I'm glad I met you too, Capri."

Against his better judgement, he stroked his free hand through her silky hair. She nuzzled his chest in response. The ache in his heart intensified. Why did he torture himself like this?

Still staring at the final sliver of the sun on the horizon, Capri spoke softly. "Eden?"

A long pause hung in the air before he could answer. "Yes, Capri?"

"I—I've had something on my mind over the past week. It's kind of silly. I wasn't sure if I should do it, or *how* I should do it. In fact, I've never done anything like it before." She turned to look him in the face.

Eden's heart beat faster. *Oh, man. Is this it? Is she…going to kiss me?* For once, he'd started to hope that she might.

"The longer I thought about it, though, the more it just felt right." Capri sat up on her hip, propping herself up on her hands to face him.

The tickle of butterflies in Eden's stomach returned as her soft hair danced alluringly around her shoulders in the sea breeze. His eyes darted to her lips, which blushed with a beauty reminiscent of the hibiscus blossom she'd kissed earlier that morning. Somehow, without even trying, she managed to break his heart.

Capri bit her lip as she took a deep, slow breath, relaxing her shoulders and lengthening her graceful neck to look him in the eye. "Eden, I—I want to give you something to express my gratitude for saving me." She leaned forward and placed a hand on his chest.

Eden swallowed. His heart hammered so hard he was sure it would burst through his ribcage.

"Eden, I…" Capri's voice dropped to an intimate whisper, her face hovering so close, he could feel her breath against his skin. "I want to give you a wish."

A mix of relief, confusion, and a hint of disappointment washed over him. It left him stunned, barely knowing what to say. "A…wish?"

"Oh, I'm messing this up, aren't I? Sorry, I'm just so nervous," said Capri through a jittery laugh.

"No, no! You're doing fine," said Eden, trying to be the brave one for even half a second.

"It's just that I—I've never granted a wish before."

With the pressure of a kiss off the table, Eden found the courage to brush the flyaway strands of hair out of her face, running his thumb along her cheek where the thin cut on her face had nearly finished healing. This seemed to help calm her nerves because she closed her eyes and took a deep breath.

"Thank you," she said. "I have to admit, I've never *wanted* to grant a wish. Humans never gave me any reason to trust them. I've never even imagined granting any of them a wish. But…you changed that for me. You're a good man, Eden. Now, I feel that the time has come. I want you to be the recipient of my—" She caught her breath for a moment, barely believing what she was saying. "The recipient of my first wish. You can ask for anything you desire."

Eden sat back on his hands, steadying himself. This was almost too good to be true. "Anything at all?"

"Anything. Choose carefully, though. The only real limitation is that I can only grant you *one* wish. I can grant as many wishes as there are people in the world, but no human can make more than one wish."

Eden shook his head in amazement. Could this be real? He didn't believe in fate, but it was starting to feel like somehow, some way, the ocean had set him up for this exact moment.

"Are you sure?" he said.

"I've thought long on this," said Capri, playing with a rough pebble she'd found. It did little to obscure the trembling of her fingers. "I want you to have this if you'll accept it."

"Oh, I am. I mean, I will. I just…wow! A wish." Eden's mind went blank. Around a friendly campfire dare, he could have come up with at least a dozen things to wish for up front, but with a real wish on the line now, he couldn't think of one thing.

Well, he did have *one* thing he longed for most. His gaze wandered back to Capri, looking her up and down as her scales glistened with a starry shimmer in the last of the sun's direct light. Oh, the things she made him feel without doing a single thing. His very soul could have crawled out of him just to hold her tender form in his arms for one more day. No other craving had ever been so excruciating in his life.

"I—I…" The wish became entangled in his throat.

"You must be overwhelmed," she said. "You don't have to answer right away. Why don't you think on it, and you can tell me tomorrow."

"Okay." He nodded, relieved. "I-I could use the time."

"For tonight, though, will you take me back home to the sea?"

"I'd be happy to," he said, though *happy* was a bit of a stretch.

It was a struggle for Eden to make the short climb back up the cliff. Although Capri added nearly no extra weight clinging to his back, his legs were unsteady. He brought her back to the small hidden beach, illuminated by the nearly full moon. Just before he set her into the surf, Capri wrapped her arms around him as she had the previous night.

"I liked our last date together, Eden. I like you."

Those words robbed him of speech. He tenderly returned the hug. "I do too. I-I mean, I did too. I'll come back at the same time tomorrow."

"I'll be waiting."

Chapter 10

Eden's Wish

That night was restless for Eden. Minutes felt like hours as he tossed in bed until he could take it no longer. He strode out into the darkness of the lonely courtyard. Not a single light was on. Only cold stripes of moonlight spilled through the slats of the latticed roof. The pool was as heavy and as still as a thick sheet of glass. It was only hours ago that Capri had been in this very space. He hadn't even moved the pocket knife or the bucket with the empty oyster shells from the corner of the pool.

Ugh, I need a swim.

Eden pulled off his white tank top, which was still briny from the beach. Wearing his beach clothes to bed had felt juvenile of course, reminding him of his stubborn insistence as a child to keep wearing his damp, worn swim trunks to bed so that he could be ready to go swimming again first thing in the morning. Eden smirked at the memory. He'd always loved the water. Some had even joked that he was so infatuated with the sea, he would probably end up marrying a mermaid.

Ridiculous, he thought, shrugging away the impossible. Still, deep in his core, nothing that anyone said would change how he felt about the water. Swimming was as liberating as it was—dare he think it!—romantic to him.

Tonight didn't feel all that different from those days. He brought the fabric of his tank top to his nose, inhaling the familiar, briny scent of the sea. A second unfamiliar scent clung to it as well. It was barely describable, but the nearest he could decipher was something like a subtle, sweet marine blossom. He knew without a doubt that the scent belonged to Capri. It sent a pleasant shiver through him. Or was it the night breeze gusting over his bare skin?

Casting the shirt aside, Eden dove into the stillness of the pool. A long rectangle of moonlight illuminated the bottom as it shone through the oculus overhead. He didn't usually go for night swims without the lights on, but this was like entering a different time-space where his thoughts were clearer and life slowed down.

Eden closed his eyes, picturing Capri swimming somewhere beneath him on one of their evening swims. Automatically, he began to imitate her graceful, fluid undulations, similar to the kick of the butterfly stroke he knew so well. For a moment, it felt like she'd never left the pool. As soon as he opened his eyes though, he was reminded of his loneliness.

The pool and garden were so empty. So lifeless. So incomplete without *her* at the center of it all. Resigning himself to the silence, Eden floated on the water with his face to the moon. Part of him hoped that Capri might also be looking upon it, waiting for his wish.

A wish. What an impossible opportunity. It was as thrilling as it was terrifying. Whatever he asked for, it had to be worthwhile.

What does *one ask for when one can wish for anything? How would it come to pass?* He could ask for the usual wishes that were always mentioned when these hypothetical situations were proposed—world peace, an end to hunger, the eradication of disease, clean oceans, and so on. And yet, somehow, it didn't feel right to say any of those things.

Only one thing kept coming to mind over and over again. He kept replaying his moments with Capri on the sea cliff. He thought of how they had both carved their initials, creating an accidental permanence of their relationship. He thought fondly of her exquisite beauty and how she had so trustingly rested her delicate frame against him. That confidence—that complete trust—contrasted sharply with her admittance of never having had a reason to trust humans in the first place.

An old saying spoken by his parents bubbled up to the surfaced of his thoughts: "A heart with even the smallest amount of faith and hope will create more beauty, change, and peace in the world than a passionate, bitter heart ever could." Although life had jaded him since last year's events, it was an oft-repeated phrase that had shaped him over the years. It had given him courage and focus whenever he'd doubted himself…kind of like right now.

An idea thrummed in Eden's head. *Could it be that simple?*

He toweled off, took a proper shower, and changed into fresh clothes for the night. With a refreshed mind, he crawled into bed as the threads of his wish were beginning to weave together. Yes. He knew what he wanted to wish for.

Eden couldn't be bothered to sleep in. He committed to his morning swim and a quiet breakfast beside the pool where Capri had usually joined him. The first half of his day was spent on routine pool maintenance and tending to the garden. Then he ran a few errands he'd neglected for the past two weeks while entertaining Capri. All the while, he thought on his wish, rehearsing his words over and over again to make certain he was asking for the right thing in just the right way.

Any time he encountered people on his errands, he became keenly aware of the use of the words "I wish." It hadn't occurred to him how overused this tiny phrase was amongst human beings. Sometimes it was over frivolous or lofty desires, like the store clerk muttering that he wished for unlimited money, or the young woman eyeing a passerby's sculpted physique and lamenting to her friend that she wished she had a body like hers. Other times, the wishes were over things that would have otherwise been in the person's control at some point in time, like the stressed-out mother in line at the grocery store, wishing she hadn't put off shopping for her family gathering later that day, or the man glancing anxiously at his watch as he hurried to his car, wishing that he'd set an alarm so that wouldn't have forgotten his appointment.

Eden couldn't blame them for their worries and longings, but the more he listened to people's wishes, no matter how sincere or shallow they might have been, the more certain he was of the wish he was about to make with Capri. Evening couldn't come soon enough.

By the late afternoon, Eden could hardly wait any longer. He ate an early dinner, hopped into his truck, and drove back to the sea cliffs. Once he'd made his way down to the hidden beach, he sat at the water's edge. The time alone with the sea felt like a necessary prelude to his meeting with Capri.

"Hi there," he said to the ocean as it washed over his feet. "I, uh, don't know if you can hear me or if you're… alive. *I* think you are. There's a universe of secrets down there most of us can't even fathom. Capri is one of them. I'm—" He lowered his voice to a whisper. "Don't tell her this if you can speak to her, but I like her. A lot. Okay, more like—I'm in love with her. Ugh, that feels so weird to say out loud. I really shouldn't be though. But…*don't* tell her I said that. If anything, *I* should be the one to say so. Well anyway, I hope I've taken good care of her for you. I think I have. Whatever happens after I make my wish, I promise to take good care of her." Eden chuckled to himself. *Why does this feel like trying to convince a protective father if I can take his daughter out on a date?* "I'm ready to speak with Capri now, if there's a way to summon her or however that works. It's no trouble though. I can wait for her. I'll always wait."

The tide was rising, but he stayed where he was of his own volition as the water rushed past him. It was just him and the peace of the sea. The balmy breeze combed its fingers through his hair and brushed his skin like a looming embrace. The longer he sat, the more he imagined nature itself to be romancing him.

Just as the sky was beginning to change color and the water rushed up to his waist, a familiar shape washed up in the next foamy wave.

Capri! The strange stir of the sea rippled with tentative excitement in his chest. The surf carried her to where he was waiting, sliding her up beside him where she gracefully pushed herself up on her hands to meet him face to face.

"Hello again, Eden," she said with an almost melodic voice.

He had to work the words out of his throat. "Hello, Capri."

"You came."

"As promised."

She arched an eyebrow. "You're early."

"So are you."

Her smirk broke into a full smile. "I know. I just had the feeling I needed to be here sooner."

Maybe the ocean did *summon her. Hopefully that's all it did.* "How was your first day back in the ocean?"

"Wonderful. I'd missed it so much. It's good to be home. Though it was very different not being near you." Her voice fell as she spoke. "I woke up this morning forgetting where I was for a minute, and I was a little sad to not be having breakfast with you."

"Aw, I missed seeing you this morning, too."

"What did you do all day?"

Eden shrugged. "Maintenance, gardening, errands. Just human stuff."

"I see."

Eden could feel her veiled giddiness because the ocean in his chest had turned from mild ripples to a lively, choppy dance.

"So," she sighed with an edge of nervousness. "Have you thought of your wish and what you want to ask for?"

"I have. I know what I want to wish for."

"Good!" she said. A flutter of excitement filled her chest. "Listen, I know this might be a little much, but would you take us up to the cliffs again? You know, where we watched the sunset yesterday. I want to watch it again since I have the chance. You can make your wish there."

"I'd be happy to take you," said Eden, turning his back to her. "Climb on."

He thought he'd be accustomed to her touch by now, but his heart still raced when she wrapped her arms over his shoulders and coiled her tail around his waist. When they made it to the lookout point on the sea cliffs, he set her down, and they settled in to watch the beginnings of the color sequence across the sky.

"It's still so different from up here," Capri gushed. "Even the sea appears to change color like I've never seen at sea level."

"I'm glad you like it." Eden glanced over his shoulder at their initials, barely a day old. It felt like they'd been there so much longer.

"Alright. I shouldn't delay things," said Capri, turning her attention to Eden. "When I have asked you what you want to wish for, simply say my name followed by the words 'I wish,' and state your desire in full. Easy enough?"

Eden nodded.

Capri squared her shoulders, lengthened her neck, and cleared her throat before speaking more formally. "What wish can I grant you, Eden?"

As steadily as he could, Eden placed a hand on hers and looked into her eyes, those beautiful, soft eyes that had seen everything that the ocean kept secret from the human world. Ignoring his pulse pounding in his ears, Eden spoke in a sure voice, never having been more certain of anything in his life.

"Capri, I wish to entrust *you* with my wish. I'm sure there are many things you'd wish for, many things you want to know and do. I trust you. You have a pure and innocent heart, and I want to hand the wish over to you to make a free choice. I leave it in your hands."

Silence enshrouded them. Capri could hardly speak. Of all the things he could have asked for in the world, he freely handed it over to her.

A sharp, whispered breath escaped her lips. "No other creature in the world has ever bestowed such trust upon me like this. Are you sure?"

Eden shrugged, grateful to finally have the wish off his chest. "The words have been spoken. Take-backs aren't actually a thing once something has been said. I would presume the same is true of wishes."

Her head swam. "Well, you're right, but this is just…"

"A lot?"

Subtle expressions took turns shifting across her face—confusion, surprise, curiosity, worry, then confusion again. What was she supposed to do with a wish?

"Was deciding on your wish *this* hard?" she said, bewildered.

Eden couldn't resist a chuckle. "Yes and no. It was overwhelming at first, but when I stopped overthinking things, it just kind of came to me. Everything about it felt right." He let her absorb what he said before adding, "You don't have to answer now, you know. Just think on it."

Capri nodded and settled for watching the sunset in silence for the next hour, unsure if she would be able to appreciate its glory with all the thoughts racing through her head. Eden was right about the many yearnings of her heart. She wanted to relish the coasts once again. She wanted to enjoy the sea as it was intended to be, free from human refuse and left to flourish in peace. She wanted humans to leave the sea alone. For that matter, she would have been happy to see humans disappear altogether. But as she glanced at Eden bathed in the evening glow of the sun, her spite for humans waned and a deep-seated iciness began to melt.

She regarded his figure with curiosity. It might have been the way the wind rustled his dark hair, or how he closed his eyes as he inhaled the coastal breeze, or the way his chest rose and fell with that deep breath, or even the way he propped his arm on his bent knee so contentedly as if he were lounging in the comfort of his own garden and wasn't perched up on a high cliff. Whatever it was, a warm feeling had begun to stir deep within her. Something about him had transformed over the past two weeks. Or perhaps the way she saw him had changed.

Has he always been this…handsome? she thought. She traced the firm contours of his body with her eyes, really seeing him for the first time. His beauty and virtue must have always been present. Her prejudice against humans must have simply blinded her. She hurried to face the sunset again before he could notice her studying him.

I've been looking inward for too long. It's time I looked beyond myself. She sat up a little straighter as her wish became clearer in her mind. She knew what she wanted, but she also knew what she needed to wish for.

Closing her eyes, she took a deep breath and enunciated her words: "I wish…that the two of us experience each other's worlds in the form and manner in which the other experiences it."

Eden whirled in her direction the moment she'd pronounced her first words. He tried to comprehend their meaning, but he couldn't be sure.

"How's that?" he said.

The last drop of sunlight dipped into the sea when Capri opened her eyes. There was a resoluteness in them that he'd never seen.

"Please," she said, taking his arm, "can you take me back to your pool again for the night?"

"Uh…yes, of course. But why? I'm not sure I understand your wish. How does it work? What happens?"

Capri looked almost as lost as he felt. "I've never granted a wish before. I'm not entirely sure how it works, but what I do know is that for a wish to begin taking effect, the person who made the wish must fall into unconsciousness."

"You mean, go to sleep? Why?" He was becoming more baffled by the minute.

"All I know is that it has something to do with what happens at the point where the conscious mind gives way to the subconscious. Something happens at the moment when the two meet. Thought and desire intersect, and the wish manifests into reality at this bridge of consciousness. Sorry if that's too vague of an explanation."

"It sort of makes sense," said Eden. "I'm still not sure that I understand it."

"I don't think it's meant to be understood as much as it's meant to be followed."

"Alright, I can take a hint," said Eden. "But go all the way back to my house?"

"Since we are joint recipients of this wish, I know that we need to be in close proximity to one another. But I wouldn't make you sleep on a cliffside or next to the cold ocean surf if it could be helped."

"Fair enough," he said.

Something had shifted in the atmosphere around them. A silent energy buzzed between them when he had her climb back onto his back, as he carried her up the cliff, and all the way to his truck to drive home once again. They were silent the whole time, but he ruminated on her words, pondering their meaning and speculating what might happen.

Once Capri was settled in his pool, he stretched and mustered a yawn. "Alright, I'll go to bed now. Any idea what'll happen after I'm asleep?"

"I guess we'll find out together," said Capri, smiling up at him with wonder-filled eyes.

Something about the way she said this suggested that she at least had a clue as to what might happen when the wish came to pass, but Eden didn't press her any further.

"See you in the morning, then?" he said, turning on the garden lights for her.

"Until morning."

Eden tossed and turned even more than the night before. He was like a child on Christmas Eve, prickling with excitement over the mysteries of tomorrow. When he became too warm, he pulled off his shirt to try cooling off. Then he attempted to read a book for a while, but he could barely pay attention, looping through the same paragraphs over and over again. Nothing could quiet his curious mind. The wish depended on his falling asleep, and as the night wore on, sleep was an assured impossibility.

After what felt like ages, he threw off his sheets and went to the window to peek through the curtain. Capri was still awake, gazing up at the oculus over the pool. The moonlight kissed the contours of her face like a silvery cloud on a summer night.

"May as well," he said, clicking the door open. His bare skin prickled with goosebumps against the rush of cool night air, so he collected his jacket from the table before heading sheepishly to the poolside.

"I figured you were still awake," she said, coming over to meet him. "Nothing's happened yet."

"I'm sorry. I just can't get to sleep," he said, forcing his arms into the inverted sleeves of his jacket one at a time until they slipped in. As he did so, he thought he noticed Capri staring at his bare torso before shyly looking in another direction.

Is she…checking me out? he thought. *Did she do that before, and I'm only now noticing?* His ears ran hot at the idea, but he pretended not to notice.

"Do you not need to fall asleep?" he asked.

"No, just you, the originator of the wish," she said. "What's keeping you awake?"

"I don't know." He sighed, pulling up a lawn chair. "The unknown? The excitement of what might be and trying to imagine it?"

"A wish comes from a place of desire rather than imagination," said Capri. "Well, I suppose imagination is needed to formulate the words for a wish, but desire is primal. It lies beneath the conscious mind."

"If you're trying to sound fancy on purpose to bore me to sleep, it won't work." Eden smirked. "I don't think I could ever fall asleep listening to your voice. It—" He checked himself before admitting any feelings out loud. "It's too nice to fall asleep to."

"Wanna bet?" said Capri, crossing her arms with a sly grin. "I am absolutely certain that I could get you to fall asleep with just my voice."

This sounded interesting. "Really? How's that?" Eden adjusted the lawn chair to a reclined position.

"Mermaids are known for their soothing songs." She watched the interested grin vanish from Eden's face. "What?"

"Don't mermaids ordinarily sing in order to lure sailors into the water to drown them?"

Capri made a face. "No, of course not. *Sirens* do that, and I really don't know why they insist on doing so. They're so miserable! They expect the men to love them, but they drown every time. When will they figure it out?"

A small part of Eden was uneasy, knowing that she might still have a similar capability, but a wish was on the other side of sleep, and trust was its foundation. "So you'll sing a song to put me to sleep, right?"

"If you'll let me. I don't know how else you plan on getting to sleep."

"Fair point," he said. He lay himself back against the lawn chair, trying to get comfortable. "Alright, you can sing a song to me then. I trust you."

A single, clear note rang softly from Capri's lips. Her sweet, bell-like voice filled the night air like a soft breeze. No words, just tones. The pure, ethereal notes sent a calm, refreshing sensation through Eden's body. It was like having the ocean flow over him, clearing even the deepest crevices of his mind of any worries. Every part of him relaxed with each blissful note that escaped from her lips—magical, swirling tones that gradually multiplied into dozens of heavenly voices harmonizing with each other.

His breath slowed to match the ocean's rhythms, and his eyelids grew heavy. As his awareness tipped toward a sleepy unconsciousness, he could practically feel her voice as if it had taken on a physical form. The hypnotic voice breathed on him, running its airy fingers through his hair and tenderly stroking his face and neck as he sank into an abyss of weightless peace.

A smile… A heartbeat…

CHAPTER 11

HUMAN

"Psst! Eden."

Eden stirred. He slit one eye open, momentarily confused when he saw a canopy of greenery and geometric slats filled with the color of the early morning. A cold, mildly damp breeze nipped at his skin.

Capri! The memory of last night rushed back to Eden, and he awoke with a start only to be startled by the presence of a stranger.

Sitting near the foot of his chair, feet dabbling in the pool, was an attractive, fair-skinned young woman, garbed in aqua capris and a soft pastel tank top that fit her like a glove. She tossed her hair and flashed a smile that might have made Eden's knees go weak if he wasn't on edge about having a strange woman in his garden.

"Hello, Eden," she said.

He gasped. *No. There's no way.*

"I guess my voice *does* put you to sleep," she said.

"*Capri*?" Eden could hardly believe his eyes. "How? When did you—?"

"Right as you fell asleep. I had wished to experience your world in the form and manner in which you experience it." When Eden didn't respond, she added, "As a human."

"Yeah, I—I can see that," he said, still in shock.

She pulled her feet out of the water and slowly attempted to stand. "I still can't believe I have a human body. I even have human skin! It's weird not having scales. Does the world always feel this—?"

She gasped, wavering as she stood on her new legs. She swayed, attempting a recovery, but tipped over into the pool with a splash.

Without a second thought, he dove in after her, jacket and all. The screaming panic in her eyes was something that he never wanted to see again. Following usual rescue procedures, he maneuvered behind her and brought her to the surface for some air. She coughed and sputtered.

"It's okay, I'm here!" said Eden, weaving his arm beneath hers and crossing it over her to grasp her shoulder. He held her close, waiting for her frantic kicking to quiet down. "I've got you. Relax, you're safe. Let's get you out."

The baritone in his voice soothed her, and she allowed herself to rest against his shoulder as he swam her out of the deepest section of the pool.

"Alright, feel that?" he said, guiding her hand to touch the pool's textured wall.

"Yeah," she gasped.

"We're at the ledge. I'm going to help you sit on it, okay?"

She nodded, letting him position her on it. That didn't stop her from gripping the upper edge of the pool until her knuckles blanched.

"Here, I'll help you out," he said. Clambering ahead, he lifted her to sit on the pool's edge so that her feet still dangled in the water.

"You okay?" he said, rubbing her back.

The panic behind her eyes was subsiding. She nodded again, still too stunned for words.

Eden masked his own shock when his fingers grazed her wet skin. *She's actually human.*

"Still not used to the legs yet, huh?" he asked.

Capri shook her head. "Neither on land nor in the water, I guess. How do you even swim? It's like having a hinged tail that's split in two."

"I can show you later, but for now, let's get you dried off."

Eden unzipped his sopping wet jacket and peeled it off. *Guess I won't be doing the whole give-her-your-coat gig,* he thought. He retrieved a couple of fresh towels from the storage bin and draped one over her shoulders before using the other to dry himself off.

He took a longer look at Capri now while she wrung the water out of her hair. Nothing about its mystical color had changed, but he had to admit it complemented her skin and the red in her lips quite nicely. The colors of her clothing were familiar too. It took a moment for him to recognize their resemblance to her former scales. Even the seafoam green and light aqua in her tank top imitated the scale patterns she'd had previously, as though the ocean had custom-tailored her clothes. Was it magic that gave her these clothes? How did it all work?

When she gathered the ends of her tank top to wring water from it, his brow furrowed at the sight of her exposed midriff and the continued absence of a navel, even as a human. In a way, she was even more otherworldly now than when she had been a mermaid. Before she could take notice of him, he averted his eyes and took to drying his own face and hair to avoid any embarrassment, unaware of her equally brief examination of his own body as he did so.

Now that she had flesh of her own, Capri began to see Eden in a different light. If she had begun to think of him as handsome yesterday at the sea cliffs, now it was as if something had shifted in her perception. Objectively, nothing had seemed to change about him since last night. He was still as tall and athletic as ever.

As her gaze wandered down the shape of his familiar figure, something about the lines of his sturdy, masculine makeup made him appear surprisingly…attractive. Like in the way a mer might find a potential mate attractive. But she wasn't into him like *that*...was she? Her cheeks began to feel like they'd been warmed by the sun, and a strange flutter writhed in her stomach. She'd never felt anything like it. *Is this a human feeling?*

Eden finished drying his face, draping the towel over his shoulders. He furrowed his brow when Capri touched her face, which flushed pink. "You alright? Your face changed color."

The pink in her face became redder. "Uh, it's fine. I'm fine. Just—"

"Embarrassed?" he said, trying but failing to hide a mildly satisfied smirk. *Guess she knows what that feels like now.*

Capri became flustered. "I-I-I don't know what's happening to me," she stammered as she felt her heartbeat accelerating. *What's wrong with me?*

"Don't feel bad." He beamed. "Many young humans have fallen into the pool before they've learned how to swim. It happened to me too when I was a kid. Your legs are new to you, so don't be too hard on yourself."

Capri loosened the tension in her jaw, but her legs felt as floppy as her tail on dry land, and it wasn't because they were new to her. Sure, she'd been a little embarrassed at requiring rescue from the pool, but it seemed Eden hadn't suspected her blushing to be about something entirely different. Maybe she should keep it that way, at least until she could figure out what these sensations meant.

A smile cracked the rest of the tension in her face. "Thank you for rescuing me. Who knew you'd come rescue me twice?"

"It's what I do," he said, wringing the water out of his jacket. "I can have these clothes washed and dried in a couple of hours." He stalled when he noted her wet clothes. "Um, I don't suppose you'd be willing to borrow some of my clothes while I get yours washed and dried."

"You wash clothes? Oh, wait, that's a silly thing to ask. Of course you do. Um, sure, you can wash my clothes." She looked at him expectantly. "So…what am I supposed to do now?"

Eden racked his brain, trying to think of a better way to instruct her to remove her clothes without sounding creepy. "Uh…how about we head inside for this?" he said. *No need to say anything that would make any neighbor's ears perk up with worry or curiosity.* "Don't bother walking just yet. I can carry you in."

He strained a moment as he lifted her unfamiliar new body mass, but he carried her inside his home for the first time.

Capri grimaced, pulling the towel closer around her shoulders at the bite of the air-conditioned house on her wet clothes.

"Oh! Yeah, it might be cold in here," said Eden. There were so many everyday things that he was suddenly mindful of. Stacks of unsorted paper and laundry from the past two weeks took up the kitchen chairs. "That won't work. Eh, we'll start you over here," he said, taking her to the foam tiles near his workout area staged in the corner of the living room. *Probably better than a wet couch or the cold floor*. The only carpeted spaces were his bedroom and the soft rug on the living room floor. His bedroom was out of the question as far as he was concerned.

Once Capri was seated on the soft tiles, she watched Eden hurry to close the door and draw all the blinds for privacy.

"Wait there a minute," he said before disappearing down the hall.

She listened to him open a door and head into a room on the other side of the wall, shuffling for a minute before returning with some dry clothes in hand.

"Here, change into these," he said, handing a half-folded T-shirt and basketball shorts to her. "They'll be big on you, I'm sure, but it'll be just until your clothes are washed." Then he handed her a linen laundry bag. "You can put your wet clothes in there."

Capri took the bag, a confused line creasing her forehead as she tried to interpret the meaning of his words. "Ooohhh, so you mean I need to take my clothes off."

Eden shifted uncomfortably at those words. "Uh, yes, that's right. Wait! No, not until I leave the room." He'd whirled away from her just as she was beginning to lift her shirt.

"Oh, okay. Sorry," she called as he disappeared into the hall.

Out of sight, Eden slumped against the wall, closing his eyes and rubbing the bridge of his nose with his fingers. *It's fine. You're fine. You didn't see anything. You're fine,* he thought, dialoguing with himself. *Relax. It's not like you haven't seen her…figure before.*

Yeah, but she's always been clad in fish scales and colorful patterns.

You were fine then. But no, the minute she has skin, you freak out.

Look, I don't know what changed after she became human.

It's because she's unreasonably attractive, isn't it?

I mean, yeah, she's…easy on the eyes—

"I put the clothes *in* the bag?" called Capri.

Eden's stomach lurched. "Uh, y-yeah. Yeah, just put them in the bag and put on the dry clothes."

A beat of silence, and then, "Okay."

His internal judge laughed at his discomfort. *Wow, you're twenty-two years old, but you're as jittery as a teenager who's never even kissed a girl. Well…almost never.*

He rolled his eyes at himself. *Look, Jess was all handsy and clearly had one thing on her mind, and so many others have been creepy like that. But Capri is different from other girls. She's got an innocent mind and heart. I trust her.*

"I'm done," called Capri.

A muscle twitched in his jaw. *You sure about that?* his internal judge sneered at him.

He squared his shoulders. Still, his knees quivered as he rounded the corner of the hall and into the living room.

There she sat, wearing his black T-shirt and his basketball shorts that matched her lips. They were so oversized, they made her limbs look extra spindly and fragile.

"Uh…are you…comfortable in those?" he said.

"Yes. They were a little tricky to put on, but I figured it out."

"Good. Don't worry, you won't have to wear them long. I'll get our clothes washed up, and you'll be back in your own clothes."

"I don't mind all that much. I kind of like them." She brought a corner of the shirt's collar to her nose and inhaled deeply. "They smell like you."

Eden chuckled behind a wince. "I hope that's a good thing."

She didn't answer as she kept the fabric pressed to her nose.

Unwelcome images of other girls who had done the same to his shirts in an attempt to flirt with him at the pool came sauntering through Eden's mind. He had never felt more uneasy and embarrassed than when girls did this, especially when they knew he was watching them do it. But the girl sitting on his living room floor was nothing like those girls.

"I'll go change," he said, collecting the linen bag. "When I get back, I can clear the kitchen chairs for us and warm you up with a fresh cup of coffee."

Chapter 12

Breakfast with a Mermaid

Capri wasn't terribly impressed by the coffee. It was more bitter than she was used to, but she liked how it warmed her from the inside after the sharp cold of wet clothes. The blanket around her shoulders made her feel something she couldn't put into words.

"Cozy," said Eden as he finished preparing food in the kitchen. "It's where you're warm and comfortable on the inside and the outside. It often involves eating or drinking something warm and wearing something insulating to stay that way."

"Huh, cozy," she repeated, snuggling into her blanket at the kitchen table where Eden had placed her. She quite liked this new human feeling. She'd figured out how to fold her legs over each other like she'd fold her arms while perched on the chair. It was nice to be able to warm her own toes.

"Alright, while we wait for the laundry to finish, I'm going to serve you some breakfast. If you don't like any of it, I promise I have some shrimp ready for you."

"You're too good to me, Eden," she said. The smells wafting through the air made her mouth water, so she had a good feeling about the food he was preparing.

He set a fresh tray of food on the table. "Well, it's your first time as a human, and you deserve the best. Okay, now here are some things that humans eat for breakfast. Right here, we have scrambled eggs—chicken eggs, that is—and pancakes, oatmeal, toast, and some honey to go with it. Then here are a few fruit options. We have orange slices, strawberries, and grapes."

Capri's eyes widened at the display before her. It looked strange, but it also smelled enormously good. She couldn't figure out how to use a fork, so she used the spoon meant for the oatmeal on the eggs, which she tried first.

"Oh, these are so moist!" She took a few more bites before trying the oatmeal. It wasn't her favorite texture, but it sure tasted cozy. The pancakes were surprising. They were soft, but hearty, and the thin drizzle of runny syrup made them extra tasty.

"They're specialty protein pancakes," explained Eden. "Most people eat pancakes that are less dense than this."

"What makes these so special?" she asked between bites.

"It's the protein in them. It's complicated, but it's a nutrient that helps muscles grow and stay healthy."

"Like yours?" she said, scanning his toned biceps.

"Um, yeah." He could almost feel her curious gaze physically brushing his arms.

"I imagine human muscle works like mer muscle, right? It helps you move through the water?"

"Yeah, swimming through the water, walking and running on land, really any kind of movement."

"Walking, huh?" she said, pausing to enjoy the mouth-watering sweetness of the fresh strawberries. "Oh, these are so good."

"I'm glad you like them," said Eden, spearing a couple of berries with his fork. "I honestly didn't know what to expect, whether you would dislike the food or savor it like a human."

Capri swallowed her bite of strawberry. "Per the wish, I'm experiencing your world in the same way you do. I'm still a mermaid, so things look and feel very new, but I can enjoy it as much as a human can."

"Speaking of which, how did it all happen last night? Becoming human, I mean."

Capri smiled fondly. "It happened quicker than I imagined. I remember singing to help lull you to sleep. It must have worked because you were more relaxed than I'd ever seen you. You even had a little smile on your face. Just as you faded off to sleep, right there in the pool, the water took on a mind of its own. It…did something to me. I couldn't say what exactly. Sorry to disappoint. All I know is that I had a sudden intuition to climb out of the pool, and as I did, my scales vanished like they were left behind in the water. I was left with soft human skin and human clothing in my scales' colors."

Eden tried to picture it all, but didn't know what to imagine.

"You still have a question," she prompted. "I can see it in your eyes."

"I was just thinking about how the wish works. I know that sleep is needed to 'activate' the wish, but is there a time limit? Will you be a human indefinitely or for a shorter amount of time? When does the wish end?"

"I don't know," she said. "A wish follows the design of its speaker. Neither of us really said anything in regards to time. It may stay this way until something happens regarding our experience of the other's world."

"About that," he said, "what exactly had you meant by the two of us 'experiencing each other's worlds'?"

"What does it sound like?" she said, making a surprised face when she bit into the orange wedge.

"I'm not asking right. Um…how do I say this? If something has happened to you in this wish, does that mean that something has happened to me? Or that something *will* happen?"

"It's unclear," said Capri, finishing the citrus. "Think of it like this: when you stated your wish, you rooted it in trust. So, anything that followed the wish would be built on that foundation of trust."

"Okay, I'm with you so far." He nodded. "What does *that* mean?"

"It's not clear if or how will come to pass, or if it's already happened. There's a lot I don't know about the specifics of how wishes work. I've never seen one granted before now. All I know is that you'll experience *my* world in the same manner in which I experience it."

Eden was trying to piece things together. "So you're saying that at some point, probably when I go to the ocean, I'll be…" His stomach dropped. If what he was thinking of was true, the idea thrilled him as much as it terrified him.

Capri leaned forward. "You'll be what?"

Eden could barely form the words. "I'll—"

A muffled buzz sounded from down the hall.

Eden shot to his feet. "That's the laundry. I'll load it into the dryer, and we'll have fresh clothes in under an hour."

Capri shook her head as he hurried off. A grin pulled at the corner of her mouth as she chewed on one of the grapes. *He's so funny when he gets nervous.*

Eden returned a few moments later with the sound of a different machine running. "It's the dryer," he said, pointing a thumb over his shoulder. "Human technology. It's pretty cool. Anyway, what were we talking about?"

"Walking," said Capri, sipping her coffee.

"Oh! Yes, of course, walking," said Eden loudly, relieved to avoid thinking about the intimidating effects of the wish on himself. "Yes, how about I show you how to walk. It'll be helpful if I'm going to take you into town."

Capri's face lit up like a child who was promised a trip to a theme park. "I get to see a human town?"

"The best way to see it is on foot. Here, we can practice on the rug." He rotated her chair so that she faced the living room. It was a smaller living space, but to Capri, it felt large enough that any distance felt impossibly far.

"Alright, let's start with standing," said Eden. He held her hands, and with some effort, she stood on her feet. "How do you feel?"

"A little scary, but so far so good," she said, squeezing his hands whenever she felt like she might fall.

"Great. Now, I'm going to hold your hands and walk backwards while you walk forward. You'll put your weight on one leg and bring the other forward. Okay? Here we go."

He took a half step back, leaving enough room for her to bring one leg forward. She wavered, but managed to complete the movement.

"There you go! You're doing it," he said.

"It's a lot harder than you humans make it look," she said through a nervous laugh.

"You're doing great, Capri. Now try the other leg."

The space fell silent as Capri focused on her next step, mirroring his backward step.

"There, you've got it. It's natural. You're walking like a human. Come on, let's take another step."

With each step, Capri's grasp on Eden's hands softened. They crossed the room several times. Her excitement was palpable.

"I think I'm starting to understand how legs work," she said as she gained confidence. "I want to try walking on my own."

"Should I stay here in front of you?" asked Eden. "Or should I turn around if I'm making you nervous?"

Capri rolled her eyes and snickered. "I don't get nervous like you do."

"Hmmm, we'll see about that." He stood ahead of her, arms crossed in a dare.

Capri shot back a determined grin and took a step independently, wavering but managing her own recovery. Then she took another step. And another.

With every step, Eden's smile widened. She was actually doing it. "Not bad. Remember to look ahead, unless I'm distracting you."

"Psh! *You're* the one who gets distracted."

She wobbled and took a couple of frantic steps forward, which turned into a fall. She swung her hands to catch herself but landed squarely against Eden's chest.

"I've got you," he said.

Capri half coughed, half laughed at her clumsiness, but lost her breath as she righted herself, suddenly aware of his hands around her waist. They felt protective. Strong.

Kind. It felt louder than when she'd had scales. Skin made the world feel so much more alive. A flutter returned to her stomach.

"You sure you don't want me to turn around?" he teased.

She set her forehead against his chest, chuckling. "Let me try again."

CHAPTER 13

FAKE PEOPLE

By the time the laundry was dry, Capri was walking freely around the house, fascinated by the many textures and temperatures under her feet. One surface was soft and fluffy, and the next was cold and hard. For every observation she voiced, Eden's senses seemed to fling wide open. If their conversations had made him notice the simple parts of life, now sensory elements had become more fascinating. More alive. More beautiful.

After they had changed into their clean clothes, Eden had Capri apply some sunblock to her arms, legs, and face before heading out for the morning. "Trust me, you'll need it if your skin is anything like mine."

Then they climbed into his truck and drove off into town, windows down with the crisp, coastal air filling them with life.

"Where are we going?" asked Capri.

"I figured I'd take you to the park first. It'll be an easy introduction to the human world."

Capri turned her face out the window with a smile as bright as the morning, cheer brimming out of her in a short, bubbly laugh.

The tentative, gurgling ocean building inside of Eden's chest turned into breakers of gleeful excitement right as she laughed. *Yep, she's still a mermaid.*

A few minutes later, Eden parked his truck and helped Capri out of the car. Her mouth hung open as she stepped out to meet the vivid world before her. There were strange and beautiful trees that appeared much taller up close. She insisted they pause beneath the nearest one to listen to the rustling of the wind through its bizarre leaves fanning out like stiff kelp.

"It's colder in the shade," she said, hopping out into the sun and back into the shade several times.

She's figured out how to hop already? thought Eden. *Maybe the wish is helping her adapt quickly.*

"Oh, and what's this?" she said, strolling up to a tall, stony sculpture. It produced a constant spout of water from its top like a whale. The water collected in a stone basin and trickled down into several increasingly larger basins beneath that.

"That's a water fountain," said Eden.

Capri dabbled her fingers in the streams of water pouring from the sides. "It's like tiny waterfalls that sound like rain!"

"That's one way to describe it." Her unique descriptions of the world were like poetry.

"Oh! Flowers," she cried, rushing up to the blossoms lining the sidewalk and smelling every color. "Ah, they smell different from the ones in your garden, Eden. Oh, is all of that like seagrass?" She gestured to the green covering the park.

"Yeah, kind of," said Eden. "I mean, it's just grass—"

Capri had already leaped over the flowers and into a carefree run across the lawn. It was nice and cool under her bare feet. Eden followed her as she ran through the alternating spaces of sunlight and morning shadows of the trees on the grass.

"Warm, cold, warm, cold," she repeated, feeling every bit of the shifts in temperature on her skin. When she'd run in circles for a few minutes, she sprawled herself on the grass to catch her breath, staring up at the brilliant blue sky.

Eden caught up and sat beside her. "Tired yet?"

"No. Not a bit," she panted. She fanned her arms up and down on either side of her. The coolness of the lush grass was an impressive contrast to the warm sun on her skin. She heaved a long, contented sigh. "Oh, I was made for this. How is *this* not the best part about being human?" she asked, combing her fingers through her hair until it spread all around her.

Eden was tongue-tied. He couldn't think of anything to say with his gaze wandering over her pale skin, which practically glowed in the sunlight.

"Do I look weird as a human?" asked Capri.

Eden blinked. Her worried face told him he'd been staring again.

"Oh, no! No, no, no, not at all," he said hurriedly.

"Then why were you staring at me just now?"

"Ah, it's just that…well, I guess I'd grown so used to seeing you as a mermaid, and I'm still getting used to your human form."

She sat up and spotted a few other humans coming and going through the park—a woman in workout clothes going for a run, another woman pushing her child in a stroller, and a couple sitting on a nearby bench. These were the first humans she'd seen in close proximity since meeting Eden. She lit up with curiosity, and then another feeling that she'd never considered.

She brought her voice down to a near whisper. "Eden, be honest. How do I look when compared to other human women?"

"Oh, Capri," said Eden, turning her face away from several women who were walking out onto the green, preparing to begin a workout. "You don't need to think about that. You're *you*."

"Yeah, I know I'm me," she said, "but do I look woman *enough*?"

"Why do you ask?"

She glanced over at the group of women beginning a series of stretches. "Well, I'm afraid that I don't look enough like them to be a human. My hair isn't right, and I'm not even as pretty as them—"

"I'll stop you right there," said Eden, taking her by the shoulders. "Don't question for one second if you look enough like other people to qualify as human. You wished to live as a human, and you know what? That's a normal human way to think. Practically everyone thinks that way at one point or another."

Capri didn't seem entirely convinced.

"Let me ask you, Capri. Do you trust me?"

"Yes."

"Then trust me when I say that you really are beautiful. You never need to compare yourself to anyone. Being a woman isn't a competition, nor is being human, for that matter. Your only job is to be yourself."

"How do humans do that?"

"It sounds cliché, but it's as simple as being yourself and accepting the beauty you already have within you."

Capri mulled over his advice. "Huh, I guess that makes sense."

"Come on," said Eden, helping her to her feet. "We can talk while we walk. We still have a lot to see today. I want to take you to the pier. It's a perfect day to visit."

They walked from the park and down a few blocks until they reached a long beach on one side of the street and lively shops on the other. Locals and weekend tourists gradually appeared for a day at the beach and to visit the pier.

Capri surveyed every single human with fascination. Much like merfolk, no two looked exactly alike. The longer she considered that everyone she passed might have the same insecurities about themselves as Eden had suggested, the more at ease she became. This was especially true when she saw another young woman with hair of a similar aqua as her own, albeit much shorter.

"Am I mistaken, or are marine colors not naturally occurring amongst humans?" she asked Eden.

He caught on when he spotted the same woman. "If by marine colors you mean greens and blues, then you're right, it's not."

"So how do people like her get such colors?"

"Er, don't be too obvious," he said, gently catching her wrist as she tried pointing. "They dye it with color or wear fake hair."

Puzzlement contorted her face. "Fake? Humans do things that are fake?"

"More often than we'd like to admit," he said uncomfortably.

"Why is that?"

"Eh, it could be for a whole slew of reasons. Sometimes it's for fun and playful self-expression, but that only works if the person accepts their innate beauty. A lot of the time though, if you ask me, I think it's because we're compensating for something that we don't like about ourselves. For many of us, being fake means that we can gain people's attention and approval, even if there's something flawed in us."

"Sounds a little like lying," said Capri, disappointed.

Eden examined his own conscience as she said this, recalling the medley of times he had tried to impress people simply to win their approval or to impress them to fuel his vanity. "It kind of *is* like lying. Not to defend being fake, but I think people do things like that because they're afraid of being alone and forgotten."

The more she looked around, the stranger humans seemed. "Being fake is so bizarre. If there's one thing that's starkly different about merfolk and humans, it's that merfolk don't fake things. We can't. We are part of the ocean, and the ocean cannot lie."

"Because *nature* doesn't lie," said Eden.

"Exactly!" said Capri, lighting up. "Nature can be difficult to understand at times, but if we let it alone and listen to it, it is the Teller of Truth, and it directs our way of life."

She's quite the thinker, he thought admirably.

"I don't like how common it is for humans to be fake, though," she continued. "How do you know when they're being fake?"

"It can be hard to tell. Some people look confident and put on a happy face, even when they're upset. But I guess, in general, the louder they are in voice or in appearance, the more fake they tend to be, like they're trying to distract or hide from the truth."

As he spoke, an uncomfortable knot formed in his stomach, recalling the evening he had smashed the glass in the courtyard. Although he hadn't outright lied to Capri when she'd asked about the stupid thing he'd done, a part of him felt fake for keeping a pertinent slice of his past hidden from her.

If she knew what I'd done, he thought, watching her observe the world around her, *there's no way she'd trust me. It would break her, shatter everything we've built. No, I couldn't do that to her. She doesn't need to know.*

"Hmmm…loud," continued Capri, taking him out of his thoughts. She contemplated the attributes of people around her. The woman with aqua hair sure had looked "loud." A pair of skateboarders had bright, metallic outfits and body paint that appeared as loud as their dynamic movements. The man behind the wheel of a flashy car was especially loud as he revved the engine when he drove by. The harsh noise made her flinch, and she took hold of Eden's arm.

She began to feel sorry for some of these people. The longer she looked, the more their loud facades melted away, revealing their insecurities.

A pang of sadness stung Capri's heart when she spotted one particular woman leaning against a fence post while doing something on the phone in her hands. She had a beautiful face, but a distinct sadness flickered behind her eyes. Maybe even a hint of worry. Not a single human seemed to notice that pain. Her revealing outfit, which left very little to the imagination, commanded people's attention far more than the grief in her eyes.

Does no one see how upset she is? wondered Capri. *Then again, would anyone bother asking what's making her sad when she's hiding behind clothes that talk so loudly?*

Capri wandered toward the woman. "Excuse me, are you okay?"

The woman's face pinched up, surprised by the question, and yet the blend of worry and sadness in her eyes was unmistakable. "Uh…yeah. What gives?" Her tone was sharp, like she'd been rudely interrupted.

"It's just, you looked sad, like something bad had happened to you, and I thought—"

"It's okay, Capri," interrupted Eden, taking her by the arm. Then he said to the woman, "Sorry, didn't mean to interrupt anything." He pulled Capri along before the woman's glare could turn icy.

"I like your face! It's beautiful, you know," called Capri over her shoulder as Eden hurried her away.

"Why'd you try talking with her?" said Eden in a soft voice.

"Why didn't *you*?" said Capri, like he'd missed the most obvious opportunity to perform a good deed. "Didn't you see how worried she looked?"

Eden was embarrassed to admit that he'd noticed everything *but* her face up until the point when he was guiding Capri away from the interaction. "I thought she sounded upset about being interrupted."

"No, she was sad and worried. But the rest of her appearance betrayed what she was really feeling. I don't know why she would try to become faceless when she was in so much distress. She had a beautiful face, too. I think more humans would have wanted to help if they'd seen her face. But when she presented herself so loudly and so fakely—that's a word, isn't it?—she gave herself less of a chance to be seen. *Really* seen. She deserved some friendly help."

Eden's lips pressed into a line. He stole a glance over his shoulder, catching the woman crossing the street with a hand over her mouth, brow upturned, and a tear running down her face as if she'd never been told she was beautiful. Maybe she hadn't!

Eden stared back at Capri in amazement. Where he and other humans saw bodies and loud expressions, she had seen souls longing for connection. "You know what? I'm proud of you, Capri. Humans can get stuck in the noise and facades, but you see the people behind it all. I've gotta say, humanity could learn a thing or two from you."

"Really? I'm learning a lot from you and all of these people." She could feel someone eyeing her as she spoke.

When she looked ahead, she spotted a young man jogging towards them. He was impossible not to notice as his shirtless torso gleamed with a sheen of sweat, rippling with muscle.

A spark ignited a small fire in Eden's gut as the man intentionally slowed his jog to look Capri up and down before shooting a wink at her as he passed. Eden instinctively, though unconsciously, took her by the hand. *That's the fifth guy who's eyed her this morning. Even in modest clothes she's undeniably attractive.*

"Was he another fake?" she asked.

"It's anyone's guess. Some people work hard to look like that, and others take steroids to—"

"What does *this* mean?" she asked, holding their interlaced fingers up at shoulder level.

Eden was so jarred by the change in topic, and even more shocked that they were holding hands, that his words tangled. "I—wh-what? Hand holding?"

"I've seen other humans doing it all morning, but not everyone. It's usually two people like us. Why are they doing that?"

Anxiety crept up Eden's shoulders as he scrambled for an explanation. How was he to describe this without suggesting any romantic feelings for her, but also without lying? "It's often a sign of trust between two people. It's a little like they're saying, 'I'm here with you no matter what, and I won't let anything happen to you.' It's a loose definition, but that's the gist of it."

"Oh," she said, wiggling her fingers in his. "Is that why you took my hand?"

"Ah...yeah." Eden squeezed her hand in affirmation. "No matter what."

CHAPTER 14

THE PIER

Capri rather liked the feeling of Eden's hand in hers as they made their way down the beach. The longer he held it, the more natural it felt to her. She squeezed it as they arrived at the pier.

"It's so much longer than it looked from far away," she remarked.

The shift from cool concrete sidewalks to the rough wooden planks beneath her feet astounded her. They were touched by the same sun. How could they have such different temperatures? She admired every texture she found on the pier, from the cold metal of the light posts, to the chipped paint on weathered railing, and the glass on the windows of the shops dusted with traces of sand and sea salt. The air was filled with strange and wonderful scents mixing with the brine of the sea.

"It's getting close to lunchtime," said Eden. "Want to try a different kind of human food?"

"Only if it's as good as your cooking," said Capri.

"Oh please, it's not that special. I was going to take you to the juice bar at the end of the pier. I saw how much you liked those strawberries this morning, so I have an idea of something you might like there."

Capri's eyes twinkled with excitement. She waited on a bench while Eden spoke with someone at the window of a shop decorated with splashes of bright colors and cutouts of colorful fruits. After a couple of minutes, Eden returned carrying two transparent cups with a strange material in them, one of them a soft red, the other a pale yellow-green.

"Here we are," said Eden, handing her the red one along with a spoon.

She eyed it cautiously before taking it from him. It was cold and slightly wet on the outside. Its contents were like liquid snow. Something about the cup and the spoon didn't feel right to her.

"Are you alright?" asked Eden. He thought he spotted a twitch in her eye.

"Mostly. Um, what is it?"

"It's like a smoothie. It's strawberry with blended ice and nothing more. Give it a taste. Try using the spoon while it's denser. I think you'll like this one."

Capri cautiously scooped up the smoothie with her spoon. It proved almost too cold for her mouth, but after a few spoonfuls, she adjusted and became enamored with the flavor. "This is just like the strawberries from this morning, but in a different form. I can even see the seeds." She drew one out from the side of the cup and examined it on the spoon.

"Do you want to try mine?" said Eden. "It's lemon-lime. It might be a bit strong for you, but—"

"May I remind you that I'm experiencing the world as a human does," said Capri with a daring grin. "If you can handle it, I'm sure I can."

Eden went back to the shop window to request a smaller spare cup. Upon his return, he poured a small amount of his smoothie into it. "Alright, give this a try."

Capri's brows bounced at the sharp citrus flavor. "It's like the orange slice from this morning, but stronger." She took another small spoonful as she adjusted to the flavor. "Not bad. Though I wonder…" Taking her strawberry smoothie, she poured a nearly even amount into the smaller cup, mixing it with the lemon-lime before trying a spoonful of her concoction. Her eyes went wide at the taste.

"You like it?" said Eden.

"Why didn't I do this sooner? Here, taste it," she said, nearly shoving the spoon in his mouth.

"That's *really* good," said Eden, eyes widening at the burst of the sunny flavor. "I'm going to have to mix these two flavors more often. Good choice, Capri."

For a while, they sat on the pier enjoying their smoothies and their elevated ocean view. They watched people come and go, completely unaware of the mermaid in their midst.

Capri watched one particular fellow finishing his smoothie while standing at the pier railing. When he expected no one was looking, he dropped his empty cup over the edge and into the water, then turned to leave as though nothing had happened.

Capri was aghast. Images of the thick layers of refuse along the coast flashed in her memory. "I knew there was something I didn't like about these cups," she said, flinching away from it like it had stung her. She shot to her feet. "I've seen them before. They're treating the ocean as a catch-all. That's my home! How could—?"

She stumbled over her own feet in an attempt to run to the railing to see the damage done. A few people eyed her but continued about their business as Eden came to help her back up.

"Hey, it's alright," he said in a hushed tone. "What he did was wrong, but what's done is done. You can't change what he did."

"That's my *home* the humans are destroying," she said, bending over the edge of the pier to see the plastic cup floating away in the water.

Eden could feel a raging tropical storm churning in his chest as her long-harbored wrath for humans came bubbling to the surface. It frightened him.

"Not all humans are like that," he said. "See? Look over there."

A young woman further down the pier was just finishing her smoothie, and she tossed her cup into a large blue cylinder container before continuing about her business. Capri hurried over to the cylinder and looked into it. Inside it was not just one but several dozen empty plastic cups.

"It's a recycling bin," said Eden when he caught up. "It's where people throw out their used plastics, which can then be made into something else later. Here." He handed over her empty plastic cup.

Capri reluctantly took it, held it over the bin, and dropped it inside with the others. She had seen so many other cups like these littering the surface and the ocean floor around the pier, but it was so different seeing them contained like this.

"And here all this time, I thought these cups served no purpose whatsoever," she said.

Another man finishing his drink passed by and tossed his cup inside the bin, followed by another couple who threw theirs in as well. Capri was amazed.

"You see, humans aren't *all* out to litter the ocean," said Eden. "Many of them have the common sense to keep garbage out of the water."

"How could that be when I find so many countless items in the water?"

A thought occurred to Eden. "Here, let me show you something," he said, taking her by the hand and into a gift shop. "Why don't you point out a few things in here that you usually find in the water?"

Capri pointed to a woman near the checkout. "That thing she's holding."

"Ah, let's try not to be so obvious," said Eden, bringing her hand down again. "Just use your words. Okay now, you mean the thing she's holding? The plastic bag?"

Capri nodded, her nostrils flared. "I find so many of those in the water. Many creatures I've loved have swallowed or choked on them, mistaking them for jellyfish. Others have been caught in them and found dead days later."

"I see," said Eden calmly. "Tell me, what is she using it for?"

Capri watched the woman packing a few items in the bag. "To carry multiple things at once?"

"Precisely. It's a tool used for carrying things more easily."

She frowned. "Couldn't she just use her arms to carry stuff?"

"It's not always that simple. Don't merfolk do something similar?"

Capri shot him a look like he should have known better than to ask such a question. "We use what nature gave us," she said, holding her hands up. "Not even the treasure-hunters among us have anything like that. I suppose I can see the usefulness of a bag in human terms, but how in the world do these things end up in the ocean?"

Eden ushered her back outside as her voice grew louder. "Sometimes the ocean breeze will pick up an empty bag and toss it into the water. I've seen it happen many times on the beach. Some people try to catch them, but it's not always possible to keep them from winding up in the water."

"Do *you* try to catch them?"

"Whenever I can. It's part of my job to keep the beaches clean and safe."

"Can those bags be placed in that blue bin?" she said, watching another person toss a wadded paper bag inside.

"Not specifically in *that* bin, but there are places that it can be taken to for recycling. My point is that there is usually a way for things to be disposed. Come on, show me something else you find in the water."

Capri continued pointing out other things along the pier that she'd find polluting her home, while Eden would explain their intended use in the human world. They even went down to the beach to find some of these items in the sand. It made Capri's blood boil. As enraged as she was by human fickleness and carelessness, the mermaid couldn't deny her fascination over the humans' innovation.

Aluminum cans and bottles of glass and plastic were designed to transport fluids from one place to another while their accompanying plastic or metal caps were made to keep the fluid inside. Thinner cardboard boxes, rigid plastic containers, and bags lined with seals allowed food to be kept clean from external debris during transport. Paper and plastic wrappers seemed to do the same for finger foods as she watched a family sharing sub sandwiches with each other on the beach.

Eden pointed out that plastic cutlery, like the ones they had used earlier with the smoothies, was a single-use substitute for metal cutlery used for the sake of convenience. So were straws, the sight of which made Capri shiver as she recalled seeing one lodged in a sea turtle's nostrils.

They found many small items on the beach, some caught in the surf, others half hidden in the sand, collecting beneath the pier.

"Is it too much?" asked Eden when he spied exhaustion at the edges of her eyes.

"I think I'm just tired," said Capri, running her hand over her face where particles of sand and brine mingled with her sweat.

"It's alright. Let's get you home." He brought his arm around her shoulders to guide her back up the beach toward the street.

A familiar wolf whistle met his ears from somewhere behind him. Eden rolled his eyes after a second whistle and shot a glare over his shoulder to meet Mike's mischievous grin.

Of course he'd be off duty. Eden was tempted to release his arm around Capri to avoid embarrassment, but another part of him wanted to hold her closer. He set his jaw and shook his head warningly at Mike.

Mike responded with a lewd gesture, licking his lips for effect.

Oh, how Eden would have gladly pummeled the living daylights out of Mike for making such suggestions about Capri and him, but he kept his fury in check, choosing to commit his focus to her as they reached the street.

"It's not a far walk to the park where the truck is," said Eden, more for his own comfort than for hers. *Just three blocks*. He prayed Mike wasn't following them. After half a block, he hazarded a glance behind him.

"So who's the chick?" teased Mike.

Eden was so startled, he impulsively reached across to pull Capri's other shoulder close to him.

"Mike! Would you mind your own business?" barked Eden.

"Easy. I was only checking out the goods," said Mike, looking Capri up and down salaciously. "Kind of rude to not introduce your girlfriend."

Eden's stomach lurched at the word. "She's *not* my girlfriend. I was helping her out." He stepped between Mike and Capri as she shrank behind him, overwhelmed and confused.

"Then why'd you have your hands all over her just now?" Mike winked.

Eden's brow hardened. "Forget about it, Mike. I'm showing her home now."

"Showing her home, huh?" Mike's tongue rubbed the inside of his cheek as he looked past Eden's shoulder to ogle Capri, who hugged her shoulders nervously. A crooked smile stretched one side of his face as his stare locked with Eden's once again. "You, uh, got any plans on what you'll do with her? Cause, you know, with that kind of body—"

Eden's fist landed squarely on Mike's nose, which sent him staggering, leaving him doubled over, hands cupped to his face while stifling a high-pitched cry.

"Don't you *ever* degrade one of my guests again." Eden's voice burned with rage.

Mike could hardly speak against the searing pain in his nose, but his widened eyes gave away every bit of his shock. He stumbled away, while Eden hurried Capri along, arm protectively around her once again.

"Are you sure you're alright?" asked Capri, glancing at the pink in Eden's knuckles on the steering wheel.

"I've had worse," said Eden, flexing his fingers. They'd be sore for a while, but it was a satisfying soreness when it had meant defending Capri. "Trust me, I'm fine."

She chewed on her lip as the world moved past her outside the truck's window. "Who was that man?"

Eden sighed. "Some punk I know from work. He was the guy who left me that glass bottle that I smashed last week. He'd…written a rude message on it."

Capri scrunched her face as she connected Mike with Eden's pain from that grim evening by the poolside. She ran a finger over the place where her cut used to be on her face. "What a jerk."

"You can say that again. I'm sorry you had to meet him. He can be so crass around the ladies."

Capri stared out the window, replaying the interaction. "What did he mean by 'girlfriend'?"

Why did that term always make Eden's stomach flip? "I-it's a human phrase. Nothing that applies to you or me though. He was trying to taunt me is all."

"Oh." Capri had the feeling this must be one of those times he was satisfying the truth, but wasn't willing to reveal more than was necessary. His face gave it away. "Thanks for standing up for me back there, Eden."

His chest fluttered as she rested a hand on his bicep. The remnants of adrenaline in his veins combined with her soft touch was a cocktail of encouragement, igniting a sense of purpose in his gut.

He cleared his throat. "You're welcome."

She gave him a light squeeze in response. The feeling of his toned arm was as reassuring as his baritone. She didn't let go as she stared out the window again.

"I, uh…I hope the tour of the beach wasn't too overwhelming," said Eden, breaking the silence after a while.

"No, no, it was good for me to see it from a human angle," said Capri. "I'm still disappointed in human neglect, but I was surprised by how many people disposed of things properly as you showed me."

"Many of us are trying," he said. "Most people don't intend to hurt the ocean. I think a combination of neglect, laziness, and thoughtlessness is to blame for the damage done to the ocean."

"You remember that group of teenagers we saw below the pier?" she said. "You know the ones wearing those very loud clothes?"

"You mean high-visibility vests?" Eden grinned. "Yeah, I saw them too."

"Did you see what they were doing? I saw them carrying large bags and collecting garbage from under the pier."

"Yeah, we have volunteers who come through sometimes to help with beach cleanup."

"You mean they pick up garbage of their own accord?"

"Pretty much," said Eden. "I personally know of a dive team who goes out periodically to collect garbage that has collected on the sea floor. You wouldn't believe how much they find there annually. Wait, no, I think you'd know. Probably better than they do."

"I know what you mean. It worries me when some of the merfolk go treasure-hunting sometimes," said Capri, looking out the window again. "I'm all for exploration, but I'm afraid that one of these days, they'll get hurt or get themselves caught in something."

Images of the ghost net caught around her tail flashed through her mind again, silencing her.

Eden sensed her distress and tried to offer a distraction. "The sun's probably tired you out. You're welcome to take a nap when we get home. Then later, if you're up for it, I can show you how to swim in the pool."

Capri was grateful to be snapped out of a bad memory. "Sure," she said, swallowing back some tears.

CHAPTER 15

A PERFECT SUMMER AFTERNOON

Capri hadn't realized how much the sun had sapped her energy until they arrived home in the courtyard. Eden explained that the sun could give humans energy as much as it could take it if exposed to it long enough.

"It looks like it also got your shoulder a little bit," he said.

Capri winced as he lightly pressed on a pink area on the top of her shoulder. "What's that?"

"Another part of being human," said Eden. "Sunburn. Too much sun can inflame blood vessels underneath."

"Is that bad?" she said, her eyes widening.

"It's not deadly, but can be painful. Some aloe vera will help soothe it. Wait here." He had her sit on a lawn chair while he fetched the pocket knife lying near the pool, and used it to slice the corner of a thick leaf from a plant along the fence. Then he cut it open and scraped out a small amount of the clear material inside onto his fingers. "Alright, hold still."

Capri curled her lips in tightly as he applied a small amount to the burn. It immediately cooled her skin. "That's already feeling better."

"See? What'd I tell you? Oh, uh, there's a little on your nose and cheeks as well. May I?"

With an affirmative nod from her, he ran his finger over the inflamed bridge of her nose and along her cheekbones, kissed pink by the sun. Her face was so soft. He could barely focus with her oceanic eyes staring at him while he worked. He slowed his thumb over the place where the cut had been. It was healed. A tinge of remorse pulled at him.

"There," he said, wiping the excess aloe on his shirt. "How's that feel?"

"Better," she said. Her gaze was still locked on him, captivated by his touch. Why did she want his fingers to linger on her face just a little bit longer?

"Right," said Eden, looking toward the house. "Well, um, I can offer you my couch to nap on. Or, um…" He squirmed at the idea of offering her his bed.

"I'll sleep out here if it's all the same to you," she said, leaning back in the lawn chair.

Oh, thank goodness. "Whatever you like. Can I bring you a blanket or something?"

"No, I'm still warm from today, so I think I'll be fine."

"Ah, those are the best naps," said Eden, fondly remembering those summers when he would crash on the bed, his swim trunks still damp but his skin all warmed by the sun, and he would sleep without so much as a sheet covering him and wake up a short while later to the smell of dinner being prepared.

I should give her that, he thought.

"I'll be inside preparing dinner," he announced as he headed for the house. "It's nice out this afternoon, so I'll leave the door propped open if you need anything."

"Thank you, Eden. I had fun this morning." Something about the way a shaft of afternoon sunlight caught the contours of her cheek and her hair as it tumbled over her shoulder evaporated the lingering remorse in Eden's heart.

"I had fun too. Enjoy your rest."

Eden began dinner preparations, pausing occasionally to glance out the door into the courtyard to check on Capri. She resembled a sculpture of classical antiquity, lithe and fair in her peaceful slumber. He would have been happy to stare, but he pushed himself to stay busy.

Nearly an hour later, Capri awoke to the sound of something sizzling on the stove while a pleasant smell wafted through the open door.

"You're awake," said Eden as she entered the house. He was in the process of transferring some cooked shrimp from the pan into a bowl of pasta. "Did you sleep well?"

"Great, actually," said Capri, blinking the sleep from her eyes. "I didn't know I needed that. What are you making?"

"Sautéed shrimp with pasta, spinach, and capers, all tossed in a lemon garlic butter sauce," he said, mixing the sauce into the pasta.

"Heh, not sure why I asked," said Capri, clueless as to what most of those words meant, but the wilted dark green leaves in the dish resembled sea lettuce. "It looks good though."

"I figured you might like this recipe. This has been a family favorite every summer."

"Speaking of which, do you have a family?"

"Of course I do," said Eden, transferring the food to their plates. "I grew up here on the coast, but my parents are retired and live in a beach house further north. I have one younger brother in college. I'm the only one here, but I don't mind it. This house was actually a rental property that belonged to my parents. I offered to take up residence here when they considered selling it, and I've been maintaining it ever since. So yeah, that's my family story. Not much to tell."

Capri nodded, not understanding much beyond "parents" and "brother."

"Dinner is served," he said, carrying the plates to the table where cutlery and water glasses were already set. "How about you, Capri? Do you have any family?"

Capri explored her food a bit as she spoke, challenging herself to try the fork this time. "Merfolk call their pod their family, though 'pod' is the more common term. We're not always related to one another. Some of us are born into a pod, other times we find our own pod who operates in a manner characteristic of a certain way of life. Some pods are treasure-hunters, others are explorers, still others are nomadic. Either way, I guess you could call us 'found family.' Mine is a more adventurous pod anyway."

"And you're the only one of your pod who's visited the coast?"

"Only three of us ever did, but I was the only one who visited regularly. Others said it was too risky. Oh, wow," she said, finally savoring her first bite. "Eden, this tastes like how summer feels."

"I hoped you'd like it," he said, raising a glass. "What about that other mer? You mentioned a name. What was it? It sounded like a series of islands or something."

"Antilles?"

Eden dinged his fork on his plate. "That's the one. Is he part of your pod?"

"Oh, no, he isn't," said Capri, getting a better taste of a very tart caper. "He's a deep-sea mer. Unlike my kind, his species are solo swimmers. He was so generous to me and my pod, probably the only one who expressed any trust and compassion toward us for our plight." She put her fork down and gave Eden a long, intense look. "You have been just as compassionate to me too, Eden. Maybe more. You took me into your home, let me live in your pool while I recovered, and you gave me your wish of all things. No one has ever given me as much as you have, and I'll never forget that. Thank you."

"Oh, of course. I don't think I'd have done anything differently." He could tell that she had something else to say, but she resumed eating, keeping it to herself. "Uh, after dinner, would you still like to try swimming in the pool?"

She hummed in agreement. "Then could we visit the beach to watch the sunset? I'd like to see it again."

"Whatever you like. You're my guest."

After their early dinner, Eden changed into his swim trunks before taking a few minutes to tend the garden as he usually did while Capri dipped her feet in the pool, trying to psych herself into swimming with legs instead of a tail.

"You know, you don't have to swim if you don't want to," said Eden, removing his gardening gloves.

"No, I do. It's part of the human experience."

"Alright. I'm done with the garden, so we can—"

Capri splashed into the shallow end of the pool, fully clothed.

"Or we can do it like that." It wasn't like he had any appropriate swim gear for her anyway.

"I don't have what those other girls wear," she said, adjusting her tank top. "Besides, it kind of feels like I'm still wearing my scales with these."

"Whatever helps you," he said, removing his shirt and climbing into the pool.

Capri suddenly felt shy. She couldn't tell if it was because she was being re-taught how to swim, or if it had to do with him baring so much skin while being so close to her, especially while she had human skin of her own.

"You ready?" he asked, coming closer.

She could only nod.

"We're going to start with something simple. Hold on to the edge of the pool and let yourself float up like this."

Capri did as he said. *So far so good.*

"Good, now move your legs like you're walking, back and forth." He demonstrated with his own legs, slowly and steadily.

Capri used more of her knees on the first few kicks.

"Try to use your whole leg. Avoid arching your back."

She tried again, struggling as she sank.

"Hang on, let me help you," he said, coming around to her side to support her hips. "Okay, I've got you. I won't let you sink. Now, focus on your legs."

A blush crept into her face at the feeling of his hands on her hips. Taking a breath, she focused on kicking with her whole leg.

"There, you're doing it! That's much better," said Eden, lighting up with pride.

Capri smiled to herself. He was as good at teaching her how to swim as he was teaching her to walk.

"Now, if you can, hold your breath and put your face in the water. This'll give you a better feel for what swimming feels like. Yes, like that. Now keep kicking as you go."

Capri immediately felt the urge to hold her breath with her face in the water. So many times she had stared at the bottom of this pool, breathing as easily as she could the air. How did this feel so starkly different?

"Whenever you need air," said Eden, "try rotating your head either left or right and take a breath when your mouth is above water. Take it easy, I've got you."

His instructions are impeccable, she thought, turning her head to take a breath.

"There you go! Now, face back underwater and hold your breath until you need air again."

They continued like this for a couple of minutes until it became more natural for her.

"Can I try moving across the pool now?" she asked.

"Oh, you're ambitious," teased Eden. "Okay, you'll keep your arms out in front of you, one hand on top of the other like you usually do. Just remember to keep kicking. Try swimming the shorter length of the pool. I'll be right next to you."

Capri let herself lie flat, face down in the water, arms extended, and she tried kicking. She thought she was doing pretty well, but she always felt like she was sinking and losing control of her buoyancy. She felt Eden tap her back, prompting her to stand again.

"You're arching your back again," he said. "Can I try supporting you?"

"Uh, sure," she said, backing up to where she started. Walking through water was stranger than walking on sand. "Okay, ready."

She lay flat on the surface, surprised and strangely intrigued when Eden's hands came to assist her, one supporting her by the hip, while the other slipped under her stomach, pressing her up toward the surface to correct her arching back. Her chest fluttered with his body so close to hers.

"There, now try again," said Eden.

With his support, Capri began moving across the short end of the pool. Just by his touch, she felt like her ability to swim had been restored. She even held her breath longer than she would have expected.

"You've got it, Capri. Do you want me to let go?"

Never let me go, she thought. Wait, had she actually thought that?

She turned her face to the side for a breath and gave a quick "Uh-huh." His hands slipped away from her as she propelled herself forward with her legs.

"You're doing it!" she heard him say proudly.

She could still feel the places where his hands had been, like he was still there. Her form aligned, and she was swimming across toward the deep end of the pool. Out of the blue, below her appeared Eden, facing up toward her, changing his swim from a mirror of her own to the dolphin kick he was so good at, undulating his chest and hips while keeping his feet together. She mirrored him as best she could, feeling a familiarity in the full-body stroke. Just like that, it all made sense. It was like being mermaid and human all at once.

"Well, Capri, you did it," said Eden. "You learned how to swim like a human. How's it feel?"

"It's how I'd imagine flying to be," she said through a pant.

"Why else do you think I swim?" said Eden.

Capri let her extended arms cut just below the water's surface as she rotated her torso back and forth to create some waves. How had water managed to become so entertaining as a human?

"Oh!" she gasped. "Can you teach me how to use my arms now?"

CHAPTER 16

THE MERMAID'S LAMENT

The hidden beach was barely a ten-minute walk away from home, so at Eden's suggestion, they decided to go there on foot later that evening. Capri insisted that they not miss this sunset. She was excited to try climbing down the steep slope on her own instead of holding on to Eden, so he held onto her hand as they descended.

"How was that?" he asked when they reached the bottom.

"It wasn't as difficult as I expected," she said, catching her breath more from the thrill than from fatigue, "but still, maneuvering with two legs takes a lot of focus—woah!"

Eden had swept her off her feet and into his arms.

"Then I guess I'll have to give your legs a break," he said with a grin that would have made her knees buckle if she had been standing.

Why did she keep feeling like this whenever she looked at him? *Of all the human sensations and feelings, I think I'll miss this the most whenever I turn back into a mermaid.*

An unusual sadness tugged at her heart, knowing that she would have to say goodbye to Eden. It was heavier than the sadness of having to leave the coast that she loved so much for the strange waters of the deep. Nothing had made her more grieved before than that, but now she feared that her wish had unintentionally bestowed a heavier pain upon her.

"You alright?" asked Eden, noticing her distant, pensive look.

"Just thinking about how much I'm going to miss being human," she said, smiling in spite of the glassiness in her eyes. Her feet had barely touched the sand as he set her down, and she was already fighting back more tears at the feeling, knowing she would never be able to feel sand in the same way again.

She flung her arms around Eden, pressing her cheek to his chest.

"Capri?"

"I'm going to miss you so much," she said, trying not to sob. Yes, saying goodbye to him was going to be so much harder than saying goodbye to the coast.

Eden's arms wrapped around her, holding her close. He kissed the top of her head, caressing her hair, which was nearly indistinguishable from the color of the evening surf.

"I'm going to miss you too," he said, keeping his lips to her hair.

They stood there for a while just beyond the pulse of the waterline, holding each other in silence until their breathing synced with that of the ocean surf.

"You still get to watch this sunset," said Eden, breaking the silence. She turned her face up to him, her eyes glassy. "I'll watch it with you," he said, taking her hand in his. "No matter what, remember?"

A broken laugh escaped her as she squeezed his hand. "No matter what," she whispered.

He couldn't tell if this sunset would be their final goodbye, but like he had the first time, he promised himself to treat it like it was their last.

Capri dug her feet in the cool sand, very intentionally soaking in the sensations of being human, from the blissful scent of the sea breeze in her nostrils to the feeling of it combing through her hair while she watched the sun cast its orange-red light across the sky again, casting wondrous hues of blue and purple in the textured clouds drifting in for the evening.

"Never have I experienced so much beauty in one day," said Capri. "These enhanced human senses have been unlike anything I could have ever thought to wish for. You're fortunate, Eden. No mer could ever feel what you get to feel every day."

"Well, I don't know about that. Merfolk can still sense and feel things, can't they?" He couldn't tell if Capri was thinking hard or if she was merely absorbed by the sunset. "What *can* a mermaid feel?"

Capri dusted the sand from her fingers and traced them over her palms. "It's true, merfolk can sense the world, but they do not feel it inasmuch as they feel everything else from within."

"I'm…not sure I follow," said Eden.

"Joy. Sorrow. Pain. Wrath. Desolation. Can you feel them?" She searched his face for an answer.

"I mean, sure. Humans experience those feelings all the time."

"But can you *feel* them? Feel them *inside* you?"

Eden paused. Was she referring to the recurring interior sensations of the sea in his chest? Did she know about it?

"You have," she said. "I can see it in your eyes. You've felt it rising inside of you as though the sea were within you."

"I thought to ask you about that," he confessed, bringing a hand to his chest. "I've felt something like that over the past two weeks. The first time I noticed it was when I rescued you. I've only ever felt it when you're around though." He hoped she wouldn't take this as an admittance of his love for her. "Does it have something to do with you? What is it?"

"There is something about your heart," she said, placing her hand over his on his chest. "All merfolk bear a piece of the sea in their hearts. It is deep and pure, so every emotion is made tangible from within, in the secret language of the sea."

Eden was trying not to miss what she was saying, distracted by her delicate touch, a touch that he would deeply miss. "What are you trying to say?"

"Whatever the ocean feels, merfolk can feel it because they are part of the sea. You may not be a mer, but your *love* for the sea is like that of a mer so that you too can feel it."

As she was speaking, Eden directed himself to the sensation of the ocean inside his chest. He had sensed it off and on throughout the past two weeks, but now, it was vast. Deep. So full of mystery and beauty. Perhaps Capri had been something of a mediator between him and the ocean.

"I do feel it," said Eden.

"You're fortunate to have such a connection with the sea," said Capri. "If only more humans could feel it like you can."

She rested her head against Eden's shoulder as the final gleam of the sun disappeared. She hesitated to speak further so as not to disturb the rhythmic voice of the water lapping at their toes, but there was so much she wanted to say and nowhere near enough time. As the first stars appeared in the darkening sky, she finally broke the silence.

"Eden, I want to thank you for a perfect day today. I never knew being a human could be so wonderful."

"The pleasure was mine, Capri." He removed his jacket and placed it on her shoulders as he saw goosebumps appear on her arm. *Finally got to give her the jacket,* he thought as she hugged it around her shoulders.

"There was something that I never did figure out today," she said. "If being a human allows for such a beautiful sensory experience, why would some people not want to preserve that? Why would they throw garbage into the sea on purpose? Could it be that they *aren't* experiencing the world as I did?"

Eden put a reassuring arm around Capri. "I think the issue is that we don't all appreciate the world in the way you did today. It was all new to you, but...well, it becomes old and commonplace for the rest of us who spend our lives here."

Capri shook her head, incredulous. "After tasting what it's like to be human, how could anyone *not* love the ocean or even the coast? I saw those humans for myself today. They walked in the same sand, smelled the same salty air, and felt the same breeze. It was one of the happiest feelings in the world. Was that not enough? Was nature not enough? Do they not *know* what they have, what it means—what it feels like—to be human?"

Eden shifted in the sand, folding his hands while the crashing surf filled the silence after her impassioned declamation. "Unfortunately, a lot of humans take life for granted, myself included. Life has a way of dulling our senses. It's not an excuse, but a reason. Most of us aren't even aware of how the world around us truly feels. It's hard for humans to love something that they don't see or believe is real."

Capri dug her fingers into the sand. "I know it's real," she whispered. "Why can't they?"

Only the waves could tell how long they sat in silence as the moon rose overhead, illuminating the tiny, secluded beach.

Unexpectedly, Eden felt something welling up inside his chest, like a rising tide, bitter with pain. He glanced over to see quiet tears rolling down Capri's cheeks. He could make out the very soft notes of her clear voice in a wordless song that rode between the cold hush of the wind and the deep hum of the tide. The mermaid's lament evolved into multiple layers of voices like he'd heard last night. They filled the beach until he couldn't distinguish whether the song was in the air around him or in his own head. The song poured into the ocean inside of him until it spilled over the edges of his heart like a torrent of grief.

So profound was her lamenting that he became overwhelmed with sorrow and tears brimmed in his own eyes. He clutched his chest as if to stop the waterfall, but it bled ceaselessly. The sea within was desolate—devoid of living creatures, replaced by a thick, clouded wash of debris. Within this sea of misery, he could sense Capri suspended in the water, her body limp and lifeless in a hazy shroud of hopelessness. An overwhelming anguish seized Eden's heart. It was like being dead while remaining alive.

The lament felt like it stretched for ages, though it only lasted a few minutes. Time itself couldn't contain the mermaid's grief.

The hush of the tide came to life again as Capri's final note faded into the night.

Eden could barely speak. Her lament had told him all he needed to know about the pain of human forgetfulness and negligence.

"Come here," he told her, swallowing a lump in his throat. He brought a consoling arm around Capri and embraced her like he would never let her go.

The mermaid wept silently into his chest. She had sung this very same lament to the stars, longing with all her heart that even one soul would hear her. After singing it so many times, particularly at the time of her pod's exodus to the deep, she had accepted that it would have no effect on her lot. But now, for once, she felt like humanity had really heard her cry. Eden's compassionate ear was as good as the world to her. Listening to his beating heart became a kind of solace, quieting hers until the ocean inside her had calmed.

As her tears fell onto his collarbone, she saw the glinting of blue scales appear on his skin, left behind by each tear. *It's time.*

Then she said it aloud. "It's time."

"Time for what?"

Capri wiped her tears away and looked up at Eden. "Time for the remainder of my wish to come to pass. I can feel it. Go, run into the ocean. Swim as far and as deep as you can."

Eden stared out at the inky ocean. He'd never gone swimming in the night like this without preparation. He shook his head, puzzled.

"Just go," urged Capri. "All will be made clear then. I'll follow right behind you. I promise." She gave his hand a squeeze.

No matter what, he thought.

His heart pounded as he stood, brushing the sand from his legs. Then without a second thought, he raced into the cold surf.

CHAPTER 17

LEAGUES OF PARADISE

With a few bounding leaps, Eden boldly cast himself into the blackness of an oncoming wave. At first, he could see nothing before him as he paddled along the surface. Taking a mighty breath, he angled himself down into a dive where he knew the sea floor dropped. This time, however, he could actually see more of the rocks and plant life below him, illuminated by the soft moonlight.

Strange, he thought. He kept going, propelling himself through the night in a dolphin kick. Remarkably, the farther and deeper he went, the less afraid he became. Even holding his breath became as easy as it was in his many underwater dreams.

Then he felt a sensation that started as a prickle in his toes. It evolved into a cool rush of sea water as if it were flooding through his veins, starting from his feet and flowing up through his legs and his torso like a swirling storm.

It pulsed through his head and into his arms, right to his fingertips.

He swam harder and faster, like the ocean itself had infused into him an energy and stamina never experienced by humans. The energy was so palpable, the water around him seemed to shimmer with it. Or maybe that was the flash of small fishes as their scales caught the moonlight, twinkling around him like stars.

Then the familiar flash of aqua scales streaked past him. *Capri?* His eyes adjusted as the water became clearer and even brighter. She halted just ahead of him, garbed in her shimmering scales. He slowed as he approached, stunned at her beauty within her native world. Fish darted about here and there, and the occasional kelp leaf drifted through the water. He was puzzled by Capri's wide-eyed gaze as she stared at him.

"Eden," she gasped, her voice clearer than he'd ever heard it underwater. "You look…incredible."

He stopped. A weird feeling came over him. Something was different. When had he started breathing? *Breathing!* he realized. *Underwater? How? No, there's no way…*

Slowly, he brought his hands up. His stomach lurched. The blue flashes of scales he'd seen moments ago had belonged to him. He slid a hand across one arm, feeling over the smooth scales covering his pale blue skin. Daring himself to look down, he followed the two-toned patterns of light and deep blue scales trailing down his body and past his hips to where his legs had once been. In their place was a magnificent fish tail, undulating back and forth.

Did I fall asleep on the beach? Am I dreaming? He ran his hands down his sides to feel where his hips fused seamlessly with his tail. The scale patterns and fins were not unlike Capri's, but they were distinctly his own. Her description of merfolk's scales on their skin suddenly made sense. Thinking back, he'd felt more naked without his shirt as a human than he did now, clad in the strong yet flexible armor of fish scales. Still, he hugged himself, feeling slightly embarrassed by the strange feeling of his unfamiliar body.

"You can't possibly be cold anymore," said Capri.

She was right. The water had lost its biting chill and had become tolerable to him. Comfortable, even.

"How do you feel?" she prompted.

"I feel…light. As light as seafoam." He wiggled his tail back and forth a few times to test it out. It was light, yet as full of muscle as his own legs would be. The lightness of Capri's body when he'd first carried her was beginning to make more sense. "I don't believe it. A merman. When? How did this happen?"

Capri could hardly contain her smile. "It's the fulfillment of the other half of my wish, that you experience my world in the form and manner in which I experience it."

"I knew it," he said under his breath, looking himself over again. "I just wasn't sure it was possible."

He looked around, stunned that the wish had also granted him the ability to see the underwater world in greater detail, even in the dark. Not even swim goggles would have permitted him such clarity.

"Wow," he breathed. "So this is what it's like."

Capri let him take in the environment and his new body for a few minutes before asking, "You ready for some exploration?"

"Really? I mean, yeah, I guess so," said Eden in a half-bewildered laugh. "How do I, um…"

"You swam up to this point as a merman," said Capri. "You're a natural swimmer. Come on."

Doing the only thing he knew how, he extended his arms out in front of him and resumed his go-to dolphin kick. The new power in his tail astonished him. It was flexible yet powerful enough to propel his human half. In a single undulation of his chest, hips, and new tail, he launched further than he anticipated, running into Capri.

She caught his elbows as he righted himself. She snickered. "Remember to look ahead, unless I'm distracting you."

Eden grinned at her clever use of his own words from earlier. Still, he wasn't about to admit out loud how much prettier she looked as a mermaid. Her hair came alive underwater, blossoming around her neck and shoulders in a flowing frame.

Yeah, definitely distracting, he thought.

"Come, we'll go together," she said, taking his hand and giving it a small squeeze. "I'll show you how fast a mer can go."

Keeping their hands joined, Capri allowed Eden to lead as he learned to pick up speed on his own. He was easily approaching a speed that would rival dolphins. Then Capri pulled him ahead, swimming even faster so that he was nearly being towed along. Before long, they were streaking through the water at incredible speeds. Fish and smaller wildlife whizzed past them in a blur.

"Now tilt up!" cried Capri as they angled their bodies toward the water's surface, and in a most exhilarating moment, both mers leaped out of the water, soaring through the air in two graceful arcs before plunging back into the sea, bubbles dancing all around them.

"It's like flying." Eden laughed, catching his breath. How he breathed, he still didn't understand, but it was as intuitive and automatic as it was on land.

"Isn't it? Even better, I have one particular method where I *really* feel like I'm flying. It's with the giants of the sea."

Eden lit up. "You mean whales?"

Capri nodded, pointing westward toward the open sea. "We have to swim further out to find them. They're not far."

They traveled a little ways until they heard a deep, long call.

Eden shivered with awe. "Is that what I think it is?"

Ahead of him, a large silhouette approached.

Capri took his arm. "A humpback whale. He'll come to us. Just wait."

They remained motionless as the massive creature grew larger and larger as it neared, grazing along the ocean's surface. Time itself seemed to slow in its presence. In easy, gentle movements, Capri approached the creature and gave it a friendly rub. Without a word, she gestured with her head for Eden to approach.

Eden swam up to one side of its head. Ever so delicately, he extended his hand and touched it. The whale made a soft, deep purring sound that vibrated in Eden's sternum. He became lost in its great eye, a lump forming in his throat as it looked back at him. It was as if the spirit of nature itself was holding him in its sacred gaze. The whale regarded him with a docile, gentle reverence, staring deeply into his soul with recognition of all that he was, understanding that although he was not of the ocean, his heart belonged to it.

"Hello," was all Eden could say.

It seemed to smile through its eye, imparting a lifetime of words without a sound.

"He's glad you're here," whispered Capri.

"Yeah," he breathed, unable to tear away from the creature's majesty.

The whale dipped its nose further into the water to show them the top of its head.

"What's he doing?"

"He wants to give us a ride," said Capri. "It would be rude to turn down a whale's offer."

They clambered up onto the whale's head, gripping onto some of the barnacles there. The ocean shifted as the whale took off. It wasn't remarkably fast, but to hold onto its back and drift as it pulled them along was indeed like flying. When they ascended to the surface, they were greeted by the dome of the star-filled sky. Not a trace of land was in sight as they coasted beneath the heavens, just an endless stretch of sea and sky, and the deep hum of the whale as it bore them between the twin expanses where time lost its meaning.

Eden flipped onto his back for the clearest view of the Milky Way drifting overhead. Out of the corner of his eye, he spotted Capri resting on her elbows, gazing ahead, lost in the beauty of the night. His periphery became his focus until he was staring at her. The silvery moon lovingly traced her every contour, illuminating her hair as it billowed in the wind. Even her darker scales shimmered with starlight.

Had becoming a merman caused him to find her that much more attractive? Whatever the case, he locked this image of her in his mind forever. She cast him a knowing look, but in a way he didn't care that he'd been caught staring this time. He had found paradise.

"Is all of this the best part of being a mer?" he breathed dreamily.

"Depends on who you ask," said Capri. "But in my opinion, yes, this is one of the best parts."

"It's beautiful," said Eden, so enamored with the moment that he would have gladly divulged his love for her.

"It looks good on you," she said. Her compliment failed to sum up how she was feeling as she scanned his scaled body, which practically glowed in the moonlight. He wasn't quite as chiseled as most of the mermen she'd known, but the wish's transformative touch had done something remarkable to him, infusing the purity of his virtue into every sinuous line, every robust curve, and every scintillating scale that graced his body. Her stomach fluttered as she found herself unconsciously leaning toward him.

"Capri?" breathed Eden. His voice trailed off as he became lost in her gaze.

"Eden?" she whispered, her face dipping closer to his. She flicked a glance at his lips.

He swallowed as she brushed a wayward strand of hair from his face. Something behind her eyes sparked a pleasant warmth that coiled in his stomach. His jaw relaxed, lip quivering as her breath mingled with his.

"Capri…I…"

The whale's hum yanked them out of the tender moment as it descended into the open water. The mers each caught hold of the barnacles on the whale's head to stabilize themselves. Eden rolled back over onto his stomach, exhaling like he'd just been awakened from a perfect dream while Capri cleared her throat and looked off in another direction. Whatever that had been, it left Eden's pulse racing and his head spinning.

The whale came to a pause near the edge of a reef.

"What is it?" said Eden.

"Look," whispered Capri, pointing to the reef.

The silhouette of a creature emerged from amongst the coral. At first, Eden supposed it was a dolphin, but as his eyes adjusted, he realized what it was.

"A mer?" he gasped softly.

A second and third shape emerged, followed by a few dozen others. Their scales glinted in the traces of moonlight piercing the water, yielding the most magnificent colors.

"There are so many of them," said Eden. He watched them congregating in groups, laughing and chattering. He'd often imagined that if merfolk were real, they would live in underwater palaces. But no, they simply lived like all other creatures of the sea. They truly were a part of nature.

The merfolk didn't stay long and proceeded further west toward the open ocean.

"Where are they going?" asked Eden.

"They seek clearer waters. They are several of many pods who have been making the move away from the coast."

Eden frowned. "The garbage?"

"Mmhmm. Areas near to the coast are the most ideal living places, but merfolk will die in such waters. It is why we must move on."

Eden was afraid to ask. "Will you also go?"

She sighed. "I can't stay. I belong with the safety of my pod. I couldn't live near the coast even if I wanted to. My pod would never allow it. It's too deadly for us. I know it isn't much safer out there in the deep, but at least we have a fighting chance to survive with the help of Antilles."

Eden couldn't find anything to say as the whale moved them on to a quieter space near the edge of the reef, where they dismounted. He cast a final gaze into its magical eye in a wordless farewell. He could have cried as it parted from them, sure that whatever bond it had made with him, it would carry a piece of his soul through the ocean on his behalf.

"I've seen humpbacks from a distance, but I never dreamed I'd ride on one," he said.

"Aren't they wonderful? And they know where the best sights are. That's why he dropped us here. Look! They usually come when you float quietly."

"They? Who? What are we looking for?"

Capri motioned for him to lower his voice. "You'll see."

A short while passed. In the silence, Eden began to take notice of the peaceful sounds of the ocean from beneath its surface. The voice of the sea was deep and calm, enough to lull one to sleep, especially at this hour.

Just then, he saw a handful of tiny lights flickering in the water, as fireflies on a summer night. They came and went sporadically, but within a few minutes, they were emitting an ethereal blue hue.

"Firefly shrimp," said Capri softly.

"A perfect name," he breathed, as one glimmered over his open hand. It was like the stars themselves had descended into the sea. He wondered if this was how Capri had felt about the lights in his garden. "Woah, you get to see this every night?"

"On clear, calm evenings like this, yes. I quite like the bioluminescent creatures."

Eden continued turning to look about them. No photographs or videos could have captured how stunning these creatures looked to the naked eye. It was like floating in space. Their light glinted off of his scales, making them shift in color as they moved.

"I should show you the firefly squid next," said Capri. "They are also small, but such beauties when they dart around in the dark."

"Where do we find them?"

"This way," she said, taking him by the hand. "Come! There's too much to see and not enough time."

CHAPTER 18

SARK

Just as patience was required to wait for the firefly shrimp to appear, even more patience was needed to wait for the firefly squid. Capri offered him a few leaves of kelp while they waited. He'd been enjoying himself so much, he hadn't realized how hungry he'd become.

"Guess I finally get to try it." He winked.

It was crisp and remarkably sweet. Did Capri experience it like this?

When he least expected it, tiny glimmers skittered and flashed before them. It was the firefly squid! *Huh, like dinner and a movie,* thought Eden.

"If you move slowly," said Capri, "you can place yourself in their midst for something really special."

Following her advice, Eden paddled his way amongst the squid. If the firefly shrimp had been a wonder to behold, these creatures were on another level. All around him, lights darted like falling stars until he couldn't tell up from down. He twirled about, attempting to catch one.

"Oh! Eden, look out!" cried Capri.

Eden froze as the squid scattered, sensing something behind him. Either by luck or by intuition, he slipped his hand away at the very last moment, dodging a menacing set of pointy teeth that nearly grazed his hand.

Something large swam past him. Terrified, he instinctually darted to the nearest hiding place he could find, spotting a large, vertical hole in a nearby rock. He was within arm's reach when a frightening hiss practically paralyzed him with dread. A massive creature intercepted his path, blocking the hiding place while surrounding him with its long, thick body.

Eden held perfectly still as the creature slithered around him. He could hear its warning hiss from somewhere behind him. He gulped, turning in the direction in which it was circling to locate its head. The creature looked like a moray eel with its sickly greenish-brown hue, but it was significantly larger than any he had ever seen or heard of.

Something was odd about its head though. As it turned toward him in the darkness, the eyes glaring at him were positioned on the front of its head rather than on its sides. Spiny tufts of hair poked from the top of its head, and a pair of arms sprouted from its sides.

As it moved closer to him, Eden discovered that the creature was in fact a strange, knobby kind of merman with the long, snake-like body of an eel instead of a fish tail. The permanent glare etched in his wrinkly face promised pain, enhanced by a few crooked, pointed teeth poking through his sealed lips—the very teeth that Eden had dodged moments ago.

"Uh…h-hi there," said Eden, barely controlling the tremble in his voice.

The mer-eel replied with a cold, irascible hiss, baring rows of needle-like teeth as he did so. He creeped across the sea floor on his arms to inspect the cornered merman. Eden gulped as the creature circled close enough for him to make out individual ribs and bones pressing through his sunken, wrinkly torso—a sharp contrast to his long, smooth tail.

"Hmph," the mer-eel grunted as he studied Eden with a scowl capable of pinning any prey in place before his jaws even clamped. "Not real merman. Too weak." His hollow, eerie voice sent a chill down Eden's spine.

Eden clenched his jaw, praying this creature wasn't like other morays. If he was, he dreaded the second toothy nightmare of a jaw hidden somewhere behind his already terrifying first row of teeth.

The mer-eel ran his long, slimy tail against Eden's scales, eliciting a shiver from the frightened mer.

"Sark, leave him be," came Capri's voice from somewhere in the darkness.

Sark paid her no heed. "My home. Squid, my food. You, thief."

"Th-this is *your* home," stammered Eden. "There's some misunderstanding. I-I didn't mean to take anything from you."

"You *human*!" growled Sark, lunging at him, stopping almost nose to nose with him while Eden shrank away, unwittingly backing himself against the mer-eel's slippery tail.

Eden swallowed. "H-human?"

He grimaced as the mer-eel practically planted his spindly nose into his hair and sniffed deeply. "Hmph. Hair wrong color. Smell different."

"Smell? What do you—?" He shuddered as the mer-eel ran a pointy, skeletal finger scrutinizingly down the length of his stomach. His steely, unblinking stare was more knife-like than his finger.

"Mmhmm," said Sark, narrowing his eyes at Eden's as his finger grazed what it was looking for. "Have human navel. Merfolk do not."

I still have my navel? Eden drew a hand over his belly, feeling his one glaring human attribute. No, two! His hair failed to complement his scales. He should have guessed his transformation would be the exact reverse of Capri's.

The mer-eel scowled, flicking his finger like he'd demoralized himself just for touching Eden. "Ugh! Scaled fake. Wicked mer-killer. False. Fake. No trust."

"That is *enough*, Sark!" bellowed Capri, finally managing to weave between the two and driving the mer-eel back. "Please, Sark. This is Eden. I know he's a human, but he's harmless."

"Humans dangerous," hissed Sark, glaring over Capri's shoulder at Eden, who at this point was nearly frozen in shock. "Hate ocean. Destroy with refuse. Poison waste. Fill with traps. Want me dead. Want *you* dead."

"Mind yourself, Sark. He's under *my* care. He's part of the fulfillment of a wish. I've let him borrow the guise of a merman's body for only a little while."

Sark's glower morphed into what might have been a sneer, but with so many teeth, it was difficult to tell. "A wish! His or *yours*?"

Capri bit her lip, unsure of how to answer. Merfolk couldn't make wishes, only grant them. But the fact that Sark could see right through people's facades made her uncomfortable.

Sark put an arm around her. The sight of the creature's spindly fingers around her shoulder made Eden's stomach twist. He attempted to rise, but the mer-eel's thick body folded in on either side of him, warning him to remain still. A faint, eerie pulse in the tail—probably the creature's heart—kept Eden from so much as thinking of rising again.

Okay, no need to move, he thought. *At least not while Capri remains unharmed.*

Sark cocked his head at Capri. "Why, Capri? You know rule. Fraternize with humans, doom for merfolk."

"I know, but I—" Capri flashed an apologetic glance at Eden. Or was it shame? She lowered her voice, but it was just audible enough for Eden to hear. "He's different, Sark. He's not like other humans."

The mer-eel's brow softened for a moment before knitting back together critically. He clasped her other shoulder, speaking into her neck with a hushed tone. "Lived long to know. Seen you. Young mermaid eyes. So beautiful. So naive. Infatuated. In love."

Eden's heart skipped at the word. No way he misinterpreted the whisper. Was Sark suggesting that Capri was...? *No, don't go there. It's bad enough that you're in love with her.*

"That be weakness," said Sark, louder this time like a warning. "Cost too high. Many died. Who is next? One you care? You know, matter of time." He pushed to enunciate his next words as clearly as possible. "You know your place. You must live. Humans must die."

The sentiment was like a foul stench to Capri. She looked like she might spit upon Sark or else break down in tears.

With surprising tenderness, Sark took her by the chin, turning her face toward his. His slow, cryptic speech became even slower and softer. "Capri. No excuses. Not be trusted. You know what do. Must let go."

Capri grew pale, like she'd been told that she was about to die. Her eyes grew red with the threat of tears, even underwater. She glanced over at Eden but wouldn't look him in the face.

"But he saved my life."

"Strength not in body."

"I know. It's his heart that I trust. It's true and pure like the sea."

Sark shook his head. "All humans weak. None special. All the same. He no different. Sooner, later, fail. Always."

Capri cast her eyes down as if it would help her hide from the mer-eel's warning. The tide in Eden's chest felt stuck, neither rising nor falling. He could only guess that she must feel trapped between two choices. As to what those choices were, he had an idea or two.

Finally, Capri raised her eyes to meet Sark's. "He'll be returning to shore."

Sark nodded approvingly, releasing her before turning his critical gaze back to Eden. Just as he relaxed the folds of his tail around Eden, he swept him forward with it until he was unnervingly close. Eden could barely keep from quivering as the mer-eel studied him for far longer than would ever have been comfortable.

"Eden," Sark hissed. "Humans…not trusted. But"—his voice softened—"merfolk truthful always."

Eden's brows furrowed, unsure of what to make of any of this.

"Now leave me, human," said Sark, curling the end of his tail around Eden and flinging him away. With a huff, the mer-eel slithered into the nearby hole in the rocks.

"You alright?" said Capri as Eden oriented himself.

"Yeah, I-I'm fine," he said, rubbing his arms and suppressing a shiver. "I'm okay. I was just…surprised by him is all."

She ushered him away. "It's my fault. I should've known better than to bring you anywhere near Sark's territory. You must excuse him. He's a loner and doesn't speak much, and I promise he's not as vicious as he looks. He's nearly blind, relying on touch and smell. It's pretty common for him to get up in your face for a better look at you if he's never met you."

"No kidding. Well, that would explain his lack of personal space." Even shivered anyway.

"Come on, let's get out of here," said Capri sullenly. "I'm sorry I brought you here."

Eden cast one final glance at Sark's dark hole, certain he could see an eye glaring from it before following Capri in the direction of the coast. She didn't take him by the hand this time.

CHAPTER 19

EDEN'S CONFESSION

They swam in silence for many leagues. Every so often, they would spot another mermaid or merman going about their business. Eden made a point to keep his distance. After his encounter with Sark, he no longer felt welcome in the ocean. If they passed close enough to any merfolk, he would casually obscure his midriff for fear of stirring another mer's wrath in learning that a human was in fact amongst them.

"Why the hair and the navel?" he asked finally when they were far enough away from anyone else.

"What about them?" said Capri flatly.

"Why did those two things not change about me when I became a merman?"

Capri stared ahead as they swam through the open ocean. "I suppose the wish honors where you came from. It probably left your uniquely mammalian mark and your hair coloring to preserve what nature bestowed on you, and the truth of who you really are."

Those last words made him queasy as the hidden morsel of his past churned in his stomach. "I, uh…I was worried about you back there," he said, trying to change the subject.

"Worried about me?"

"Yeah, you know, with Sark. I didn't know if he was an enemy or if he would try to do something to you. I-I don't think I could live with myself if I let anything happen to you—"

"He's fine. He's no one to worry about. Just a paranoid old grump."

"Are you sure he's no one to worry about? You, uh, you seemed a little upset when he was talking to you."

"He has his own ideas and opinions."

"I don't know, I think he sounded a little like you did when I first met you." Eden immediately regretted his remarks when she shot him a glare. *Oh, stupid! Why would I say that?*

"When did *I* ever say anything that Sark said?" barked Capri.

"Back when you were telling me about how you wound up on the beach in the first place."

Capri stopped swimming, trying to recall what she'd said.

"You said that humans were all the same for destroying your home."

She shook her head slowly as she recalled the conversation. "I… don't think that way."

"Are you saying you've changed your mind?"

"I'm saying Sark is wrong." Her voice cracked as she clasped Eden's shoulders. "*You're* not like them, Eden. You have a perfect, pure heart. You'd *never* hurt the ocean. You never have."

She stopped when Eden didn't respond. "Eden?"

A terrible knowledge was hiding behind his eyes.

"I—I'm a merman," said Eden as regret began to contort his face. "I can't lie."

The blood left her face. She let go of him. "Eden? What did you do?"

He raked his fingers through his hair, trying to fashion what to say. The ocean inside channeled through him like a rip current—impossible to escape, and the only way out was to move with it by narrowing his words to the blunt truth.

"I—I did something once. I was intoxicated at the time—"

"Intoxicated?"

"I-it's when humans consume a certain type of drink which causes them to loosen up and sometimes do…stupid things."

Capri's eyes widened as she shook her head. She wanted the conversation to end right there and then, but knew she had to know. "What kinds of stupid things?"

Eden sighed. "It was a year ago. I'd just moved into the house, and one of my buddies, Jason, was turning twenty-one. That's the legal age of humans for buying and consuming alcohol where I live. Anyway, I was of age, so I offered to host Jason and some mutual friends at my place to celebrate his birthday. He's always had a wild streak, so I figured I would help mitigate the chances of him doing anything stupid on his birthday by hosting. He brought a few people over that night, including some girls. He always gave me a hard time about never having had a girlfriend, so at the time, I figured he was doing that to try to set me up with one of them, but I wasn't interested. I was vaguely familiar with a couple of them, but one girl in particular, Jess, was the creative one and brought in a large fisherman's net decorated with small seashells as a housewarming gift. Everyone was excited about it, and I had it hung along the fence to set the mood.

"Naturally, Jason and his friends had brought along drinks. Lots of them. I'd resolved to drink no more than two or three as the host so that I could run the party. We were all having a great time that night, but the later it got, the more the alcohol flowed. You see, the thing about alcohol is that it makes even the most stiff-necked person relax and accept and do things that they wouldn't otherwise do."

Eden knew that Capri wouldn't understand some of the terminology in his story, but he wasn't about to stop and explain more than was necessary, not now that he was finally talking about this out loud.

"That girl, Jess, got to talking with me during the party. The more alcohol I drank and the more she talked, the more charming she became. We kept going on and on even as people started leaving. I don't think Jason or anyone else ever said goodbye as they left because after a while it was just me and Jess in the courtyard, lounging in the chairs and losing ourselves in our drinks. Thinking back, I remember telling her at one point that I should stop drinking for the night, but as tipsy as I was, it was hard to turn down another drink from a pretty girl who kept flirting with me. I didn't want to look bad, so I mindlessly accepted each one."

Regret wrinkled his face. He massaged his forehead in embarrassment as he continued. "I'm ashamed to admit, I-I don't even know how much I drank, but it was more than enough for me to lose my faculties. Before I knew it, Jess was removing my shirt and putting her hands all over me. I imagine she would have gone for my shorts next because she started to climb on top of me. The moment she tried to kiss me, I snapped. I-I don't know how or why, but in that moment, somehow I was lucid enough to recognize that she was trying to take advantage of me. I shut her down.

"We exchanged a few drunken shouts, I think, but I ultimately kicked Jess out of the courtyard. I felt so violated. Looking back, I know I was at least partially to blame for accepting so many drinks. I wasn't thinking that at the time though. The only thing on my mind was that Jason had brought a girl to my house, and that he'd left me, his *friend*, alone with her so that she could seduce me.

"In my enraged, drunken state, I ripped down the fish net Jess had given me. I remember wanting to destroy it, so I collected it into a messy ball and stumbled out into the street with it, not even wearing shoes, just my shorts." He winced at the memory. "Ugh, I must've looked like an idiot. I don't know how I didn't walk off the edge of the sea cliffs when I got to them, but once I arrived…" Eden hesitated, longing to swallow the awful truth like vomit in his mouth. "Intoxicated as I was, I—I threw it."

A dreaded silence enveloped them as Capri realized what he'd done.

"You threw the net?"

Eden gritted his teeth. "I—I threw the net into the ocean so that I'd never have to remember Jess again, not that it did anything. It was the one and only time that I ever did anything like that. I'm so sorry. If I hadn't had so many drinks, none of that would have happened."

Capri had barely even registered his apology. Her head was reeling over his revelation. She felt sick to her stomach.

"Capri, wait!" called Eden, pursuing her as she made for the surface. There, the moon shone brightly overhead, illuminating her broken face.

"If it's any consolation," said Eden, "I haven't had a drink since then. I vowed to never risk ending up in such a bad situation where I could be seduced and do something stupid like trash the ocean in a fit of passion. In my defense, I did confront Jason the next day, and he told me that he was fully aware that Jess might try pulling something like that on me. He'd even *hoped* it would happen, which was why he encouraged people to leave earlier in the evening so that Jess and I would be left alone. He claimed he was doing me a favor, making it easier for me so that I'd finally 'get with a girl.' I ended our friendship after that."

He'd said it. It was as cleansing as it was excruciating to reveal this awful truth about himself. The most painful part was watching Capri become so pale, he thought she might pass out right then and there.

It was all a lie, thought Capri. *Everything he's done for me…anything he's ever said to me…the way he looked at me… the way he touched me…*

She shrank away from him like he'd turned into a revolting sea monster.

"Eden, what have you done?" she whispered. "How could you? I thought you were different. You'd changed my mind and had me believe that maybe some humans were different. That *you* were different."

There was so much Eden wanted to say, but he let her sit in her emotions for a minute.

"I guess I was right all along," said Capri after a while. "Humans *are* all the same. They're all weak. Sark said it well: sooner or later, they'll let you down. They'll fail you. I just didn't want to believe that a kind heart like yours would ever be capable of—" A lump caught in her throat as pained tears burned down her cheeks.

"Capri, I'm sorry," said Eden. He'd never felt more helpless knowing that any gesture, no matter how kind, would only inflict more pain on her. "Being drunk is no excuse for what I did to the ocean. I—I allowed myself to bend to human respect in order to be liked. I became... fake."

"Fake. False. Just like all humans become fake." She was starting to sound like Sark. "For all I know, you've been fake just to get me to accept you."

"Believe me, Capri, I wish I could go back and undo all of that—"

"One wish!" said Capri sharply. "You had *one* wish, Eden, and you blew it. You could have done something important with that wish. You had your chance to go back and undo it all. But you didn't."

But I chose you, he thought, too broken to say it aloud. Nothing he could say right now would sway her icy resentment. Except for maybe one other thing. He spoke as softly and as kindly as he could.

"Capri, show me where the garbage is on the coast. I need to see it for myself."

She pierced him with a glare as sharp as Sark's. "Why? To punish yourself? As penance?"

"It's part of your world, and I've seen what it's done to you, how it's hurt other merfolk. I can't change what I did or what any human has done, but I think it's only fair that I experience it as you have. Besides, wasn't that part of your wish?"

An hour ago, Capri would never have allowed Eden to experience the dark realities of her world if she could help it. He had looked so happy earlier this evening, so beautifully perfect under the moon with those flashing blue scales and that magnificent tail. Now that whole facade was falling apart. She couldn't care less if he tasted the scourge of her world firsthand. In her seething indignation, a part of her *wanted* him to get a good taste of his own wicked handiwork.

"Please, Capri," said Eden. "Tell me where to find it, and we can call it a night."

The mermaid's tears hadn't stopped, but her countenance had become cold and bitter. She raised an arm, pointing at the faint glow barely peeking over the starry horizon. "There. That's your home. Go. See what you've done. Then I never want to see you again."

The words were like a sledgehammer to Eden's chest. He looked between the coastline and Capri a few times, hoping to hear any other parting sentiments. Her cold eyes promised silence.

"As you wish, Capri," he rasped.

The last thing he saw of her was her arms crossed over her chest hugging her shoulders and the curtain of her moonlit hair shrouding her face in darkness with only the briefest flash of her red lips as they trembled. Whether in rage or in grief, Eden couldn't tell.

It didn't matter at this point. The sea inside him was darkening and growing cold. He sensed that his time as a merman was nearing its end.

CHAPTER 20

RETURN TO THE COAST

Every thought raced through Eden's head as he made his way to the coast on his own. Could he have said anything to help Capri understand the truth? He should have kept his mouth shut in the first place. But how would he have pulled off a lie as a merman? Immersion within nature itself, the Teller of Truth, drove him to speak honestly. Could he have omitted certain parts of the story to soften the blow? He couldn't think of how. It didn't matter anyway. What had been said could not be unsaid.

"I'm sorry," whispered Eden, hoping that the ocean could hear him. "I did something stupid, and I can't take it back. If only I'd kept my mouth shut. I lost her trust. I—I lost *her*." He swallowed a lump in his throat. "I didn't even get to thank her or tell her that I love her. But I know we were never meant to be together. That was always impossible. I just wish—"

He caught himself. There was no wish to be had. A fleeting thought of wishing to have never met Capri skittered temptingly through his mind. He waved it off.

"I'm glad I met you, Capri. Even if I never see you again, I'll never forget the lessons you taught me. I would have liked to end things on good terms. Instead, I broke your heart. I can only hope you'll forgive me one day, not for my sake, but for yours."

Upon approaching the coast of his hometown, Eden cautiously made his way along the sea floor toward the pier. He wasn't even all the way up to the shore, and he was already cringing at the medley of refuse stuck in the sand—plastic cups, aluminum cans, glass bottles, plastic utensils, straws, old ropes and chains, wads of fishing line, plastic bags, cigarettes, and hundreds of other pieces of trash that the surf had carried out. He could barely identify some of these items in all the clouded mess. It was far worse than he'd ever imagined.

He proceeded along the coast toward some of the beaches. Some areas were better than others, but the tide pools where he'd found Capri were egregious. There he found many of the same things in the nearly pitch-black water, along with other lost items like hats, glasses, keys, goggles, beach gear, clothing, and even nets partially buried in the water. The sight of some dead fish caught in the net wrenched his heart.

"Oh, Capri. This is so much worse than I imagined," he murmured.

The longer he looked and the more he found, the more he could feel the woe of the sea writhing inside his chest as it cried for help. It welled up so thickly in his throat that he feared he might choke.

When he could hardly stand to see it any longer, he made for the surface. Something thick began to smother him, forcing him to hold his breath. He nearly panicked as he began to lose his sense of direction. With a mighty whip of his tail, he surfaced. But he found himself rising out of a thick muck of human garbage, dead fish, and dying plant life which reeked of rot. His body seized at the putrid smell filling his nostrils. Nothing—no words, no mermaid's song, not even the sensation of the sea becoming clogged in his veins—could have prepared him for the deathscape surrounding him.

It made sense. Capri's bitterness. Sark's coldness. The collective despair of the merfolk who preferred risking death in the deep over life near the coast. It all made sense.

In the chaotic mess, he spotted a portion of net sticking out of the water. The sight of it made his blood boil. It didn't matter if it was the same one he had cast into the sea a year ago. For all he knew, that net had been carried off by the current. No, this net was a symbol, a sign of how one mindless decision contributed to the loss of not just the beauty of the ocean, but of how he had lost Capri.

Disgusted, he backed out of the foulness until the water ran clear around him. Only then did he submerge into the sea to cleanse himself of the vileness sticking to him. A shudder ran through him. His stomach churned. Rising to the surface, he rubbed his face with seawater, clearing residue from his hair and scales.

"Capri," he whispered, staring at the layer of refuse. "Oh, I'm such an idiot."

A small wave washed over him from behind. Within it, he heard Capri's sobs.

He whirled around to the open water. "Capri? Are you there?"

Her cries carried over the water. Eden's heart leaped as he hurried toward the approximate place in which he'd guessed she might be based on the distance of her cries. No matter where he looked, there was no sign of her.

"Capri!" he called.

Nothing. Then her distant sob once again.

He swam furiously out into the open sea. The urge to find her was as fierce as the pull of gravity. The sea streaked past him as he shot through the water faster than he'd ever attempted. He could hear her periodically, but he couldn't sense her anywhere.

Coming to a stop, he closed his eyes, focusing on the sensation of the sea within him. Maybe he could find her that way. Inside, the sea was dark. Desolate. Suffocating. Lonely. In the bleakness of it all, he could feel a gentle glow rising from the depths. It was alive, and it was coming toward him.

He opened his eyes and saw the glow of turquoise bioluminescent lights in the distance. They shifted and danced as they appeared to come closer. It was congruent with the glow he felt rising from the depths. Eden made his way towards them. As the distance closed, he could make out a strange shape, one unlike any he had ever seen.

"Eden?" called a voice.

"Who's there?" he called, squinting at the creature ahead.

It moved in a familiar manner. *Wait! It's a mer,* he realized. He beheld an unusually long, slender merman of the deep-sea species with a flatter, more alien face than other merfolk. Fins lined his back and fanned from the sides and end of his tail. Brilliant stripes of bioluminescent light lined his pale gray torso and arms, and continued to cascade down his tail like the arms of a galaxy. The imposing frill of lights crowning his head relaxed as he looked Eden up and down with his large yellow eyes.

"Eden, I presume?" His voice was thin and ethereal. "I've been looking for you. I am called Antilles."

"I am." Eden crossed his arm over his midriff. "Wait, like, *the* Antilles? You know Capri?"

"I do."

Eden's heart fluttered but then tripped. "She didn't send you, did she?"

Antilles shook his head. "No, I came of my own accord. I was ascending from the deep to visit the full moon when I heard Capri's voice. She's been missing for a couple of weeks, so when I heard her, I came to greet her. But then I saw her engaged in an argument with another mer, so I kept my distance. You were the mer with whom she was speaking."

"Oh, you saw that?" said Eden, rubbing the back of his neck. "How much did you hear?"

Antilles put a long, four-fingered hand on Eden's shoulder. "I heard enough to know that you are undoubtedly human, but that you also have a heart like a mer. Merfolk are always honest, and you are sincere of speech."

Eden curled his lips in. "I—I still did something terrible."

"Maybe, but something terrible happened to you too."

Those familiar words reminded Eden of when Capri had spoken similarly after he'd wounded her with the shattered glass. That look she'd given him—it wasn't unlike the one she had given the sad young woman on the beach earlier that morning, and here a complete stranger had seen his own pain. It brought a lump to his throat. It truly was the way of the merfolk to see the pain of the soul through the body.

"If I heard right, you were tricked and deceived by another human—though it sounded like a typical siren if you ask me—but Capri was too upset to hear it."

Eden nodded.

"She needs to see you again, Eden."

"I think she was pretty clear about never wanting to see me again."

"Perhaps. But what I witnessed after your departure suggested otherwise."

A faint spark of hope flickered in Eden's heart.

"After you'd left, Capri wept like I've never seen a mer weep. She sobbed as one whose heart has been rent in two."

"Yeah, because I broke her trust and her heart."

Antilles shook his head. "In the time that I have known Capri, she has never been one to cry easily. She has a strong spirit amongst the merfolk and is slow to give up what she has come to love. That's why she'd sneak away to the coast. No, Eden. She was weeping because she was struggling to let go of something."

Eden tilted his head. "What are you saying?"

"Her heart was cold before she met you. Whatever you said, whatever you did, whatever you wished for—it was enough to warm the chill. You gave her more life and meaning than you know. Her tears were quite telling. In your absence, she grows cold yet again. I don't know what she needs to be revived, but I believe you do."

Eden didn't know what Capri needed, and he certainly didn't think she needed *him* right now.

"Go back to her," Antilles urged, "if nothing else than to give her a chance at hope. That's what you are to her."

Hope.

Eden clasped Antilles' forearm, his heart pounding. "Take me to her."

CHAPTER 21

CAUGHT IN THE PAST

Antilles guided Eden through the nighttime waters, shining his bioluminescent lights at some points and silencing them to darkness at others to avoid attracting unwanted attention from predators as they left the sunlight zone. Ominous shapes faded in and out of sight. Eyes. Teeth. Long, spiny bodies. Eerie sounds and cackles echoed through the darkness, sometimes sounding so close, it made the hair on Eden's head stand up.

Yet he wasn't afraid. The very thought of Capri kept him resolute.

Huh, this reminds me of Virgil guiding Dante through the Inferno, he mused to himself. *Except this time, Dante's beloved Beatrice is lost in the Inferno. I'm coming, Capri.*

"Stay alert," said Antilles. "I doubt your eyes will so easily become accustomed to the darkness."

It was true. Eden could make out some general shapes, but details were practically a blur. "Capri and her pod had to move down here?"

"Indeed. Her pod and a few others. It may be less polluted, but it most certainly is not without its dangers."

"Does human refuse ever end up down here?"

"Everything ends up at the bottom of the sea. Where it appears, however, is unpredictable. The merfolk who come to the deep are desperate and have not yet learned of its propensity for human-created danger. In some ways, the deep is less cluttered than the coast. If you ask me, it is fortuitous that the debris on the coast is visible. At least there, one has a greater chance of seeing something *before* it ensnares. Everything down here is invisible."

Eden gulped. "Please be safe, Capri," he pleaded quietly.

Then a familiar tug pulled from deep within his chest. It was the ocean pointing him in another direction. He could only resist for so long before it became so compelling, he couldn't ignore it.

"Where are you going?" said Antilles as Eden diverted from their trajectory.

"I don't know, but wherever it is, I have to go there." It was as if the ocean itself was speaking to his soul, drawing him through its waters.

"Easy there! No need to rush," called Antilles.

"It's Capri. It has to be," said Eden. He beat his tail faster until he was cutting through the darkness, fearless and determined.

"Slow down, sir!" called Antilles.

Eden gave him little heed. A reckless hope ushered him along. Something told him that on the other end of the pull, he would be *exactly* where he needed to be and find what he was looking for.

"It's dangerous out here," called Antilles. "I implore you, slow down."

"I can't!" cried Eden. Although he was perfectly capable of easing his pace, in a strange way, he couldn't slow himself. "I'm so close!"

The pull within him grew stronger. Tighter. Taut as a rope. It snagged him and forced him to a sudden halt. He was where he needed to be, but Capri was nowhere in sight, even in the dim light.

"What is it?" called Antilles as he caught up.

"I don't know. I'm in the right place."

Antilles gasped. "Oh, no. Eden!"

"What?"

As Eden turned, the pull tightened around his torso. It wasn't inside of him this time. He looked down and saw dozens of thick tendrils wrapped around his body. The more he moved, the tighter they became.

"Ugh! What is this?" The strands were rough to the touch.

"A ghost net," gasped Antilles.

Eden's heart dropped. Images of Capri's wounded tail, the net he had cast into the sea in a rage, and the layer of refuse through which he had surfaced flashed through his mind.

"No," he breathed.

"Remain still," said Antilles. "I will fetch something with which to free you." The glow of his lights rotated and swirled into the deep until he vanished behind some barely visible wall.

The dark, eerie silence weighed heavily upon Eden like a tomb. To keep himself occupied, he tried experimenting with the net. He wedged his fingers experimentally between his scales and a rope pressing into his hip. How had this happened? The pull of the sea within him had been unmistakable. At what point had he run into the ghost net? Had the ocean betrayed him? Had it led him here to become ensnared as retribution for what he had done so long ago? Was the ocean angry at him for breaking Capri's heart?

As his eyes adjusted to the darkness, Eden began to make out more of his predicament. He'd swum into a reasonably sized net that was pinned to the sea floor by various rocks and debris. His extended arms and head had narrowly dodged a gaping hole in the net, but his chest was too broad to clear it, and so he'd been caught in its tendrils. Although his arms were still free, he'd already twisted about enough that the net had begun to compress around his chest and abdomen, making breathing a little harder. So he resigned himself to rest on the sea floor with his eyes toward the distant surface, waiting for Antilles to return.

"Capri," he groaned.

The echo of his voice against an unseen facade of rock was the only reply in the darkness. The only other sound was the passing movement of some other creature from somewhere nearby, and then silence. He rubbed the bridge of his nose as he sank into his thoughts.

"Is this what it felt like, Capri?" he said to the darkness. "Being caught in a net in the dark? I guess I had it coming. If I hadn't opened my big mouth and told you what I'd done…or maybe if I hadn't run into Sark…if I hadn't made that wish in the first place…if I hadn't thrown that stupid net into the ocean…if I hadn't gotten drunk and been acting fake that night just to gain my friends' approval, maybe I wouldn't have broken your heart, and I wouldn't be here. Huh, kind of ironic that of all the threats in the ocean, I get caught by the one thing I threw into it. Sark was more right than he realized. I'm here because I became fake. I *am* fake."

The cold silence acknowledged him. Hopelessness weighed on his chest more painfully than the net. Thoughts of Capri lying wounded in the tide pools flashed through his mind. How fragile and broken she'd looked. Yet her mysterious beauty had drawn him in, prompting him to rescue her. He replayed how he had bandaged her tail, brought her to his pool to recover in safety, fetched food for her daily, protected her from curious eyes, and tended willingly to her every need until she was strong again. He remembered how she had trusted him, poured her troubles out and went so far as to invite him to swim in the same space as her, and finally offering him the singular treasure of a wish. She'd trusted him for what he had been *doing* for her, not for anything he had done previously. Even Mr. Cuthbert's remark found its way to the surface of his despair: "You're a good man, Eden. Don't ever forget that."

"I am not fake." Eden sat up, and in a burst of renewed vigor, he began to wrestle the ropes with his bare hands. "Come on," he hissed, feeling one of them break after a good yank. He tore at them some more. "That's it, come on. Come on!"

He groped at a promising bundle of cords near his hip, but as he tried pulling what he'd thought was a loose rope, he found that another had snagged itself around his wrist, and in the process of pulling his arm up, he'd only cinched the net around his midsection even tighter.

"Agh! Is this how corsets work?" he wheezed. Breathing had become more difficult and any attempt at loosening the net was making things worse.

"Oh, Capri," he called into the darkness with what he feared might be his final breaths. "Wherever you are…I'm sorry. I know what I did, but I—I couldn't lie to you. I'd *never* lie to you, even if I wanted to. You were right; I could have wished to undo what I did to the ocean. I… I would have gladly done it, but I couldn't accept something that was *that* easy, requiring nothing of me. That's why..." He strained to breathe. If these were his last words, at least the ocean deserved to know on Capri's behalf. "That's why I chose you, Capri. You were more important to me...than any other wish I could have made. You...were worth it."

His lungs burned as his breaths grew shallower. His wheezes echoing back to him became less of a consoling voice in the loneliness and more of an ominous affirmation of the life slowly being strangled out of him. The echoes fell out of sync as he grew lightheaded. Or...was that the breath of a second creature? Had he begun to hallucinate? He shut his eyes to focus.

"Eden."

Of course the ocean would taunt him with Capri's grief-stricken voice in his final moments. Its vengeance was torturous.

"I'm sorry," he gasped, hoping the ocean would accept his apology. "Tell Capri...that I'm so...so sorry."

A pair of slender hands slipped around his jaw, and the touch of soft lips, delicate as a hibiscus blossom, settled onto his forehead.

Eden's eyes shot open. Even in the dull light, he could make out the distinctive ruby-red smile that had once made his knees go weak.

"I forgive you," whispered Capri, her voice nearly cracking into a sob.

"Capri?" he breathed.

"No time," she said. "We have to get you out of here."

She wielded the large tooth of an ancient megalodon and began sawing at the cords snagged against the sea floor. It wasn't as sharp as she would have liked, but it was the best she had. She began by cautiously cutting at one of the bonds around his chest.

Eden was dumbfounded, barely able to believe his senses. "How did you…find me? When—?"

"The ocean drew me here," said Capri. Her voice wavered like she'd been crying. "I couldn't understand why, but the pull was irresistible. Then I heard you in the darkness. I—I heard everything."

"You did?" Eden would have blushed if his body didn't feel like it was collapsing on itself.

"I did, and I believe you. Even Sark agreed—merfolk are always honest." She successfully snapped through a piece of the net, relieving a fraction of the tension on Eden's tail.

"I saw the refuse…on the coast, Capri," he rasped. "I… saw it all. I saw…what I'd done."

"Eden, you admitted to a single wrongdoing. If anything, I owe *you* an apology. I allowed my resentment toward humans to cause me to abandon all that was good and noble about you. Everything you ever did for me far outweighed any thoughtless act against the sea. I was so blinded by anger, I ignored what that human girl did to you. She tried to seduce you like a siren. I had seen that pain in your eyes that evening when you shattered the glass. Forgive me, Eden. I should never have—"

"Capri," said Eden, staring off into the distance. "That…wouldn't be Sark coming this way, would it?"

The mermaid looked over her shoulder to see the dull shape of a massive eel heading in their direction. She sawed at the net even faster until another section snapped, allowing additional space for Eden to breathe, though it was altogether marginal.

"That's no mer-eel," she said, dropping her voice. "That's a frilled shark."

"As in…the deep-sea predators…who feed on squid?" said Eden.

"And when there are no squid, they will feed on anything else, including merfolk," said Capri, switching to prioritize the nets snagging the ground.

Eden's blood ran cold as the frilled shark's haunting, toothy grin became clearer. When it came too close for comfort, Capri thrust the tooth at it, driving it away with a swift blow.

"Capri…get out of here. It's not safe," said Eden.

"It isn't safe for you either," she said, sawing viciously at the rope. She spotted a second frilled shark circling nearby. *Ugh, just our luck.* "You're easy prey. They're sensing our collective movement, but I can't stop. It's more important to get you out of here."

The moment the rope catching Eden's wrist snapped free, hope swelled in his chest. It was almost as good as breathing again. Almost.

"There! See if you can pull against the net to make it taut," said Capri. "You'll have to use your arms. Keep your tail stationary if you can."

Eden crawled along the stony sea floor, pulling against the net until it was just taut enough for Capri to continue cutting. It still cinched around his torso as he pulled.

"How is it?" he called over his shoulder.

"It's pretty bad, but keeping these taut helps." She fumbled with the tooth as it snagged on the rope. "Ugh, there are just so many."

Capri eyed the frilled shark coming closer. Just when it came in for a bite, she threw herself on the ground. It sailed barely a finger's breadth overhead.

"Be careful," gasped Eden, his chest burning.

"I'll hurry. Just keep pulling as much as you can. I can slice more of the net faster when you do that."

"Allow me to assist," came Antilles' voice. He clasped Eden by the forearms and pulled.

"Where have you *been*?" wheezed Eden, hardly able to sound as irritated as he intended.

"I'd been searching for a means of freeing you, but it seems Capri found you first. The activity of the frilled sharks in the area drew my attention."

"You're a wonderful sight, Antilles," said Capri. "If those sharks come back, would you distract them until I can free Eden?"

"I'd be honored," said Antilles.

Antilles assisted for under a minute before he spotted the frilled shark circling back. With a flourish of his lights, he darted about rapidly and drew the terrifying creature away, buying the mers a few minutes.

Eden pulled himself forward with his arms, which began to burn with the effort.

"Antilles' help will only last for so long," said Capri, more than halfway through severing the net strands. "He says that many deep-sea creatures can feel even the most minute movements in the water, which means it's only a matter of time until another predator finds us. Eden?" She dropped the tooth and rushed over when Eden faltered and collapsed while trying to pull against the ropes. "Eden? Eden, hang on!"

Eden's voice was a shallow rasp. "Leave…m-me. Save yourself…Capri."

Capri lay her head on the ground beside his gaunt face. His scales had gone pale. He was dying.

In spite of her dread, Capri spoke with a confidence Eden had never heard. "No, Eden. You *must* live. You are in love with the ocean, and the sea loves you in return. It's why your scales share its deepest colors. I know you want things to change, but you cannot change things if you're dead." She laced her fingers between his, squeezing his hand. "No matter what, remember? It's just like you said; I won't let anything happen to you. I'm getting you out of here, Eden. I love you as I love the ocean. And to save you is to save the ocean."

Something inside Eden lit up at her touch and her words, particularly those last ones. He had to survive. Capri *needed* him to survive. Somehow, it gave him the energy to rise again and extend his arms to grasp the stony floor once more to resume pulling against the net.

"Then…save me."

"I'm nearly done cutting the lines," said Capri, scrambling back to the ropes. "The moment you're free, I'll rush you to the surface and finish cutting the rest there. Can you manage that?"

Eden's ribcage and abdomen were so compressed, and his breath was so short, he was growing dizzy. Still, he managed a nod.

Antilles swept in, his lights dark and his voice down to nearly a whisper. "A colossal squid is approaching. It's awfully close. Try to keep it down."

Capri's blood ran cold. "No time," she said, cutting through several more lines all the more furiously in spite of the exhaustion in her arms. "I'm almost done."

"This is no protection for easy prey," warned Antilles.

"I would sooner die with him," she said, keeping her eyes on her work.

Eden was too focused on his breathing and pulling to pay any heed to the warm smile coming over Antilles' face or hear him remark to Capri, "Such a wonder how much a single human has changed you in so short a time."

Antilles did his best to redirect the colossal squid, but moving prey was nowhere near as tempting as two creatures stuck in one place.

"Three more cords, Eden!" called Capri. "We're getting out of here."

Eden couldn't speak any more. His entire body burned, begging for even the smallest sip of oxygen. Hopelessness seized him with a vice-like grip when he made out the large mass of the colossal squid in the near distance.

The blurry, swirling glow of Antilles' bioluminescent light cast the briefest suggestions of the immense scale of the monster. It was easily the size of the humpback whale from earlier, and its writhing arms and tentacles made it appear like a vision from hell. The creature quickly lost interest in Antilles and moved on toward its more vulnerable prey.

"One last line, Eden! Don't give up on me," called Capri as the rope slacked. Terror became her fuel as she began cutting through the thickest line of all. Every fiber was like rubber.

"I can't hold it off. Get out of there *now*!" shouted Antilles.

A mere flash of the monster's lethal eye was enough to spark the primal urge to flee, but Capri, nearly crying in terror, seized the remaining rope herself and sawed frantically.

"I'll never let you go," she panted. "Never again."

Just when the sharp spinning hooks on the squid's tentacles came into view, there was a resounding *snap*!

"You're free!" cried Capri.

Everything after that was a blur of a dream. Eden felt someone from behind grab him from under his arms. The hazy smear of a tentacle came down to seize him, but then he felt himself shooting through the water, ascending rapidly.

"Save us all, Eden," came Antilles' proud voice from somewhere below him.

With the last of his strength, Eden looked up to make out Capri's figure towing him toward the surface. The water about him grew brighter, then blurrier, then faded into nothingness.

CHAPTER 22

SAVING EDEN

The whispering of the ocean was the first thing that crept into Eden's consciousness. Then the cold of the water around him. He could hardly breathe as he felt himself being dragged through shallow water before being gently laid onto a shallow, sandy bank.

With the singular drop of strength he could spare, he slit his eyes open to see the night sky and the hazy neon blur of the moon high overhead. The tide washed over him in steady intervals as if trying to remind him how to breathe, but the ghost net retained its deathly knot around his body, allowing no more than a faint sip of air at a time. His eyes closed again as he faded in and out of consciousness, struggling for life.

As the final taste of air left his lungs, ensuring his suffocation, he heard the commotion of someone approaching on foot. A hand seized the net around his chest, and cold metal slipped between the rope and his body. A sawing motion, and then *snap*!

Eden took a greedy gulp of air as the pressure on his rib cage eased. Air had never tasted so sweet. Those first heaving breaths caused him to feel lightheaded, and a sound like high-pitched static filled his head.

"Shhh, you're alright, Eden," came Capri's muffled voice through his ringing ears. "Hold your breath a moment longer."

Eden steadied his breath and held it again as the cold metal sliced through several more ropes around his middle. *Snap*! He took another gulp of the salty night air, freely expanding his diaphragm to catch his breath.

"Steady! Steady," said Capri, resting her hand on his chest. She audibly inhaled and exhaled, slowing her breath and syncing her hand with it until it matched the surf.

Eden followed her rhythm as his hearing returned and the life trickled back through his body.

He opened his eyes. "Capri?" he rasped. "You're…human again?"

Tears of joy streamed down the mermaid's cheeks as she cupped a hand over her smiling ruby lips and nodded. Even she could hardly believe he was speaking with her. "I carried you to the surface and managed to drag you up onto the beach. I lost the tooth on the way up here, and there was nothing sharp enough to cut your bonds. You were so pale, and barely breathing. I thought I was going to lose you. That's when I understood that the wish would be complete once I rescued you as you had once rescued me. So, I crawled out of the sea and became a human once more."

Eden pressed his elbows into the sand to sit up a bit. He was still a merman. The tangled net still bit firmly into his lower waist, hips, and much of his tail. He held still as Capri gathered some of the rope strands around his waist and dexterously slipped a familiar blade between the net and his scales. When the lines snapped, Eden finally took grateful deep breaths from his belly.

"That looks a lot like my knife," he said.

"It *is* your knife. I was sure it would work faster than shells or any shark teeth, so I climbed up the beach and ran back to your house to get it from next to the pool."

Eden was almost at a loss for words. "Wow, that's... unbelievable. Thank you. You weren't hurt during our escape, were you?"

"No. Just shaken. How are you feeling?"

"I'm kind of raw from the rope, and I'm pretty drained. But I'm alive, thanks to you."

"I did what you would have done, or rather, what you once did for me. It was the least I could do."

Eden watched in silence as she worked on cutting the ropes around his hips, awestruck at being on the other side of a rescue. Capri's human hands felt so different against his scales, and as she had once described, he could feel more of her from within through the sea that dwelt there. It was as calm as it would be following a fierce tropical storm—pained, wounded, but at peace. And there was something else in it that he couldn't quite understand.

"Did you mean what you said?" he asked after a while.

Capri kept her eyes downcast, focused on a particularly difficult knot. "What do you mean?"

"You said earlier, 'I love you as I love the ocean.' Did you mean that?"

Capri stopped mid-cut to meet his gaze. Her voice caught in her throat as fresh tears streamed down her cheeks. "And to save you is to save the ocean."

"A mermaid is always truthful," said Eden.

She dropped the knife and flung her arms around him. "I meant every word of it, Eden. I admit, I'd once thought that the ocean would be better off if humans just disappeared, but that wouldn't have changed a thing. Right now, the ocean needs humans. Merfolk need people like you. *I* need you. I understand that now." She hugged him a little tighter. "I only regret that it took you nearly dying for me to finally see it and put aside my bitterness. I couldn't see what I was losing. Oh, I'm so sorry. I should never have let it come down to this. How did I ever stop trusting you?"

Eden lifted her face toward his, brushing a tear from her cheek. "Someone once told me, 'A heart with even the smallest amount of faith and hope will create more beauty, change, and peace in the world than a passionate, bitter heart ever could.' I never needed the wish to find happiness. That's why I gave you my wish, in the hopes that if you could trust even one human—even one who did something terrible to the ocean once—you might begin to understand that there are more people out there worth believing in. I was certain that this alone would bring you a truer, lasting happiness."

Years of resentment melted out of Capri as she sobbed into his chest. He held her closely, stroking her hair as a tear escaped from his own eye. "Your trust in me, Eden, means more to me than the cleanest, purest ocean. You made me believe in something I never believed existed. If it hadn't been for you, I would have died a bitter, mistrusting mermaid."

Eden brushed her tear-stained hair from her face. "Well, now you get to live and be a happier, hope-filled mermaid."

Butterflies fluttered in his stomach as she slipped a hand around his jaw and gazed up at him with eyes as glassy as the sea.

"Eden," she said, "I don't know how else to say this, but something's happened to me over the last two weeks. When I'm with you, I feel things that I've never felt before. I thought it might have been an exclusive human experience because it was more obvious then, but the more I thought about it, the more I realized that I was starting to feel these things even before the wish. I don't know how or when it happened, but I—I think I fell for the very one I thought should have been my enemy. I fell in love…with you."

Eden's heart was pounding as his eyes dropped to her lips and back to her eyes again where the very soul of the sea glistened. It was suddenly difficult to keep his breath even as his hand slid against her jaw where it fit perfectly, fingers threading through the silky hair on the back of her head and neck.

"I was afraid of ever letting myself admit it, Capri, but I—" He caught his breath as her other hand rested like a petal on his scaled chest. "I also fell in love with you."

As gently and as naturally as the tide rose and fell, Capri and Eden tilted their faces toward one another until, in a moment that only the sea witnessed, their lips met, like the sea kissing the shore. There in the moonlight, they held each other close, deeply feeling each other's souls as they imparted the secrets of the heart wordlessly to one another, listening to all that could never be said, and knowing the architecture of each other's hearts through a single, intimate gesture. In that same moment, they both understood the best part about being human—it was loving another person and being loved.

Caught up in their wordless exchange of affection, they hardly noticed the sea rise and quietly wash over them before receding in a whisper. When their lips parted, they beheld each other in the same manner in which they'd first met—Eden in his white tank top and red lifeguard swim trunks, and Capri in her magnificent aqua scales. The wish had reached its conclusion with their kiss. Love had been its resolution and the bridge between their worlds.

"You're human again," said Capri, caressing the beginnings of stubble on his face with her scaled hand.

Eden nearly blushed when he realized he'd wrapped his other hand around her waist while they'd kissed. The scales beneath his fleshy fingers were as soft and as smooth as he'd remembered.

"And you're…beautiful," he breathed. It was like going back to when they had first met, knowing that moment for the first time.

Then the rough sensation of something catching his lower legs drew Eden out of his enamored trance. In place of his blue tail were his legs, partially caught in the ghost net, and in the rising and falling of the surf, it had started catching around Capri's fins.

"Please, allow me," he said, taking up his knife to cut the net around his legs and then around her tail. Even though it wasn't the same net he'd once cast into the sea, the very act of removing it from Capri's body with his own hands felt redemptive. Cathartic. "Let's call this my apology for the net incident?"

"You've vindicated yourself many times over, Eden," said Capri, shifting her tail to assist him. "On behalf of all the merfolk, you have been more than forgiven. We believe in you now. You proved that it was never necessary for a human to be a mer in order to be so in love with the ocean. All the same for me, I guess it wasn't necessary for me to be a human in order to believe in the species' inherent goodness. I think I already knew because of you."

As he loosened the last tendrils of net from her fins, he asked the question he'd been dreading: "So, now that the wish has concluded, what happens next?"

Capri frowned and sighed. "If I had the ability to make a wish, I would like nothing better than to wish to stay here with you, if you would have me. In an ideal world, I'd have every reason to stay. But the ocean needs me as much as it needs you. Merfolk need to know that there are humans who are working to restore our home. They need the hope you've given me, and I can bring it to them."

Eden knew the answer was coming, but it didn't make his heart sink any less. "I'd have wished the same if I'd had another wish. You sure merfolk can only grant *one*?"

Capri nodded, her brow lined with regret. "Only one. I believe nature bestowed that limitation to protect merfolk and prevent humans from taking advantage of us."

"Fair enough," he said, gathering the tangled mess of net. "I'll take this up the shore to dispose of it myself later."

"Later?"

Eden stood, flashing her a smile. "Someone has to provide you with a decent send-off."

Chapter 23

The Best Thing About Being Human

Eden's steps were slow and heavy as he waded out into the water, carrying Capri in his arms in the same way he'd first carried her. This time, Capri rested her head peacefully against his chest, eyes closed, listening to the beat of his heart. How she would miss that sound. By the time the water was up to Eden's waist, she was clutching his tank top in her fist.

"You alright?" he asked.

"I'm just going to miss you so much," she said, squeezing her eyes shut.

He held her a little closer, touching his forehead to hers. "You can always visit."

"I know *I* could, but my pod won't allow it. They will be furious when they discover that I snuck off to the coast unaccompanied. Believe me, I've tried so many times to talk different merfolk into joining me to investigate the coast, but they don't take the same risks I do. I'm sure they'll have me under constant surveillance upon my return, but if I ever do manage to convince them, or maybe if I—"

Eden kissed her forehead. Her heart felt like it was being torn from her body to be left behind with him, and she could hardly bear it.

"Hey, however long it takes, Capri, I will gladly wait for you," said Eden, warmly and sweetly. With the water up nearly up to his chest, he released her tail into the water and then slipped his palm against hers, closing his fingers around her scaled ones. "I'll always be here, no matter what."

They embraced each other for a long time in the water, which had calmed to a whisper around them. Capri held him tightly, memorizing the shape of his body against hers and combing her fingers through his briny hair. Eventually, the rhythm of their hearts synced—slow and calm, pulsing with the ocean's unspoken promises.

She swallowed back a sob before speaking into his ear. "When the coasts and beaches run clear, when the coral and kelp begin to flourish, when the fish swim freely in the sea…it will hail my definitive return." She looked into his eyes. "I will never forget you, Eden."

A warmth filled her veins as his hands found her waist.

"And I'll never forget you," breathed Eden. "Every time I visit the ocean, every time I swim in the garden, and every night I look up to a full moon like tonight, I'll remember you. If saving me was to save the ocean, then to love the ocean is to love you, Capri, the mermaid the color of the sea and twice as beautiful."

Then for one final time, his lips met hers in a tender kiss, tugging into a small smile as her tail curled around his waist in an embrace. His breath caught as it found an exposed sliver of skin where his shirt rode up. The feeling of her scales gave him sweet chills.

I think I'll miss that too, he thought.

It was then that the ocean within him became one with the sea surrounding him, and kissing Capri was synonymous with kissing the sea itself. It was its own blissful taste of eternity.

Bittersweet tears streaked down Capri's cheeks as they kissed. She held his face in her hands, lovingly caressing his cheeks and jawline as she committed them to memory. The moment was as brief as it was eternal, but it filled her with a life she never could have imagined.

Late have I loved you, she thought, *but may it last forever.*

Eden's breath trembled a little as their lips parted. "I'll never forget that kiss either."

He still wasn't sure that he believed in fate, but if he was sure of one thing, it was that he had been in the right place at the right time, and because he had met Capri, she had given him his path to redemption, and he had given her hope for her kind and for all the ocean.

She laced her fingers through his one last time. "No matter what."

And so they parted—with a kiss under a full moon on a starry night in May.

Beneath the same sky of stars, after disposing of the ghost net, Eden stopped by the sea cliffs where he and Capri had watched the sunset. Despite the late hour, he wouldn't be able to fully retire for the night without completing one final task.

As he climbed down to the lookout point, he was already missing the feeling of Capri clinging to him for dear life. Still, he smiled at the memory. From the lonely niche in the cliff side, the dark sea looked vaster than ever before, like an opaque divide between two universes, both of which he now knew intimately.

In the moonlight, he found the initials *E + C* that they had etched into the cliff face. Locating the pointed shard of rock they'd used, he set it into the surface, encircling their initials in a familiar shape he never would have dreamed he'd inscribe. He sat back to admire his work. *Now,* the engraving was finished.

The faint sloshing of an ocean wave splashed within his ribcage. He placed a hand on his chest, turning to look out over the sea as it whispered something akin to a farewell.

If the feeling inside him was any indication, he guessed that Capri might be waving goodbye. He waved back at the watery expanse. The lapping of the ocean within slowed to mild ripples and then became as still as glass until it faded altogether.

"One day," he vowed. "I'll see you again, Capri."

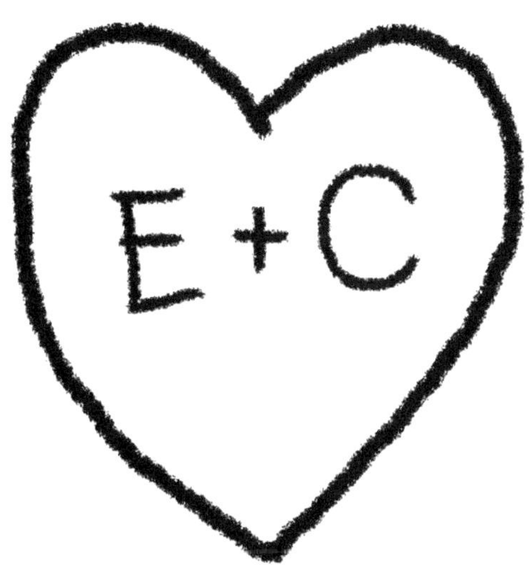

Goodbye is not forever. As the tide promises return, so does the mermaid. She dwells in the clearest of waters and haunts the sea with her song of yearning. Most never hear it, but some might chance to feel it. It is as a wordless beckoning of the sea. It fills the soul with an ache and an unfathomable longing for a serenity that nothing on land can satiate. With every wave that kisses the shore, it speaks to those who will hear it and whispers its secrets to those who will wait.

When the sea and beaches are cleared of refuse, when the coral and kelp flourish, when the fish swim freely in the sea that humans come to love again, it hails the mermaid's return.

A PREVIEW OF THE MERMAID WITHOUT SCALES

One year after Eden and Capri's parting, Eden's fellow lifeguard, Adam, hands him a glassy corked bottle with a note curled inside it. He claims to have found it washed up within the cove near the beachfront house he shares with his sister. The top edge of the note reads, "To Eden." Not knowing why, he intuits that whatever message lies within the bottle it may have something to do with Skye, the homeless girl he found on the beach the day prior. He's guessed that Skye must be on the autism spectrum like his friend Adam after the way she was behaving when he found her, and he refers her to Adam and his sister Gabby, where she stays at their private guest annex for a while until she can get back on her feet.

During Skye's stay, Adam sparks a connection with her in their shared sensitivities to sound, light, and textures, their distaste for big crowds, the need for constant stimming, and their obsessive fascination with the sea and mermaids. The more time Eden spends with Adam and

Skye, the more his guesses about who this mysterious girl is begins to shift.

When Eden finally manages to extract the curled parchment from inside the bottle, he uncovers a mysterious message from a source that he'd never imagined possible, while Adam wakes up one night to a shocking revelation. And Skye might be the key to understanding it all.

This thrilling sequel to *The Tale of Capri* promises new and familiar faces, brimming with mystery, romance, deception, and a stunning sensory journey unlike any other. Discover and experience the world of autism like you've never known it.

AUTHOR ACKNOWLEDGEMENTS

I would like to extend my deepest gratitude to the people who, in some way or another, brought this book to life. First, to former Disney Animation legend Tom Bancroft, the mastermind behind the global art phenomenon, MerMay. This book would never have existed without your genius.

I would also like to thank my beta readers Adura G, Blessing Davis, Erin Schalk, James Surprise, Karin Booysen, Madiha Shaikh, Majek Tife, and Rright Janet. Your invaluable feedback was the reason that future readers have the story they're experiencing today, with even higher stakes than the first draft.

To my incredible editor, Clara Abigail…you are a legend and a half. Your humor and exquisite care for the manuscript made the revision process a breeze. Thanks for being every bit the critic as you were the cheerleader.

I'd also like to give a shoutout to my project manager Jamie at 100 Covers. Your patience and flexibility in working with me resulted in the eye-catching cover design and beautiful formatting that readers will enjoy every time they hold this book. It's been a pleasure working with you.

A special thanks goes to the many mentors I've had throughout the process of indie publishing, including Cara Stein, Derek Dopeker, Paul Brodie, and Ray Brehm. I've learned so much from you all and I treasure every bit of your knowledge and wisdom in independent publishing.

And finally, a special thanks goes out to my husband, Alex. You unlocked something in me on that first date, and its subsequent effects are quite honestly the reason I decided to change the original publication of this book, transforming it from cute to swoon-worthy. I'm forever grateful for your influence, your support, and your love. Thank you, my beloved.

Mermay Art

Below are some of the original MerMay illustrations created for *The Tale of Capri* in 2019. They differ somewhat from the final story told here in these pages, but the scale pattern designs and general settings remain consistent with the story. As is the case with all artists, my skills have evolved over time, and although I ought to cringe at some of this older work, I'm proud of what it meant at the time and how it served as a stepping stone for me to become better than I was before.

All artwork was drawn using Copic markers and pens, and enhanced later in photoshop with light digital painting and effects.

Response to the official MerMay 2019 prompt "Stretch." This came from Capri's love of stretching herself out on the rocks to enjoy the reflections on the water. The original story started where Capri's backstory is revealed in Chapter 4.

Response to the official MerMay 2019 prompt "Nurse." This came from the idea that Eden was there to nurse Capri back to health. This was the image that started it all. I couldn't have imagined any other image for the cover of the book, and this image did serve that function in the brief but limited run of the full-color version of the MerMay story released on Amazon.

Response to the official MerMay 2019 prompt "Flight." The description was that surfing was the closest sensation to flight.

Response to the official MerMay 2019 prompt "Worthwhile." This was the moment Capri offered Eden a wish, combining the worthwhile moment of watching a sunset with making a worthwhile wish.

Response to the official MerMay 2019 prompt "shrimp." This prompt called for more than just shrimp. They needed to glow!

I lost track of which prompt this referred to as I failed to document it. However, this scene was based on a real close encounter with a moray eel. The story was shared by Don Rorschach, a scuba diver and friend who passed away in 2025. In his encounter, he very nearly lost his thumb when the eel bit him. A tooth of the eel remained lodged in his hand for life after that.

Antilles' official design. This piece was a response to the official MerMay 2019 prompt "Electric." This design was one more excuse to create a mer with bioluminescent lights.

Response to the official MerMay 2019 prompt "Run." This scene depicts Capri tending to Eden caught in the ghost net as he urges her to run as a colossal squid approaches. The final scene written in this book was far more intense than the original scene.

Yet another piece where I failed to track the prompt, so I lost track of it. Regardless, this scene depicted Capri's ascent toward the surface after cutting Eden free from the ghost net.

This scene came after the conclusion of MerMay 2019 as a bonus illustration depicting Capri's rescue of Eden after she brings him to the surface in a tide pool. The final scene in this book takes place on a beach instead for logistical reasons.

This image did not follow any particular MerMay prompt, but it was a plot twist in its own right. It was at that point that I needed Capri to save Eden somehow, and the reveal surprised even me, especially when her wish had been fashioned differently for a much shorter story so that only Eden was to experience any form of transformation.

Response to the official MerMay 2019 prompt "Kissed," when Eden kisses Capri goodbye on the forehead. This was back when I'd treated Eden and Capri's relationship as a more platonic one. It worked alright, but there was always a small part of me that wanted their relationship to be more fleshed out and complete. It honestly says a lot about who I was at the time... uninterested in being in a relationship with zero attraction to anyone. Thank goodness for therapy helping me overcoming childhood traumas. It was painful, but it unlocked something beautiful. The story you have today wouldn't have existed without it.

The final illustration that I posted for MerMay 2019. I recall that this one didn't follow any specific prompt, but it closed out the month-long challenge nicely. Needless to say, I wanted more. That's why I decided that very same summer to begin the sequel,

The Mermaid Without Scales.

About the Author

Kathleen has been writing and creating stories since childhood. Her love for storytelling eventually led to the conception of *The Color Thief*—her first independently published children's book—while studying art at the University of Dallas, earning her an honor medal for her work. Her primary writing focus is in young adult and new adult fiction. Her work frequently contains elements based on real-life experiences, exploring the deeper parts of what it means to be human and what makes life meaningful through approachable stories and imagery.

Kathleen resides in Dallas, Texas. Although she's landlocked, she relishes the daily magic of living on a lake and enjoys the occasional keelboat ride on the water.

To learn more about Kathleen's books and audiobooks, or to sign up for her newsletter to be the first to know about her next releases and purchase exclusive signed copies and merch, please visit her website at www.kathleensolis.com

Mer Glossary

All merfolk in this book's universe are named after real islands from around the world. I invite you to research these magnificent locations and learn more about these unforgettable islands that exist on our planet.

Capri is an island located in the Campania region of the Italian coast. It was Roman Emperor Tiberius' favorite island getaway and for good reason. The island is surrounded by dreamy blue waters and is the site of the Blue Grotto—a sea cave with a narrow entrance accessible only by a small boat, where the water appears to glow blue.

Sark is an island in the English Channel, just off the coast of Normandy, France. It is also known by an alternative name: "Dark Sky Island." This is because the only lights used at night are torches in order to reduce light pollution and preserve the beauty of the night sky.

Antilles technically refers to a series of islands in the Caribbean Sea, grouping islands like Jamaica, Cuba, Puerto Rico and the Cayman Islands among others. The islands are divided into the Greater Antilles and the Lesser Antilles.

A Final Word

I hope this book impacted you the way it moved me during its creation. If it did, it would mean a great deal if you took a minute to leave a quick review on Amazon, Goodreads, and any platforms where you can share your experience with other future readers. Reviews not only help independent authors like myself, but they also guide future readers in discerning if this book is right for them.

You have the unique power to shape the future of my books, and your reviews can do just that. The invaluable feedback from readers like you is the reason this book came out better than it started and it helps me know what you want to see more of. From the bottom of my heart, thank you for your support.

www.ingramcontent.com/pod-product-compliance
Lightning Source LLC
LaVergne TN
LVHW020704110826
845149LV00012B/2100

* 9 7 9 8 9 9 5 4 6 5 5 1 5 *